DOCTOR WHO
THE MARK OF THE RANI

DOCTOR WHO
THE MARK OF THE RANI

Based on the BBC television series by Pip and Jane Baker by
arrangement with the British Broadcasting Corporation

PIP AND JANE BAKER

Number 107 in the Doctor Who Library

A TARGET BOOK
published by
the Paperback Division of
W. H. ALLEN & CO. PLC

A Target Book
Published in 1986
By the Paperback Division of
W. H. Allen & Co. PLC
44 Hill Street, London W1X 8LB

First published in Great Britain by
W. H. Allen & Co. PLC in 1986

The BBC producer of *The Mark of the Rani* was John
Nathan-Turner, the director was Sarah Hellings

Printed and bound in Great Britain by
Anchor Brendon Ltd, Tiptree, Essex

ISBN 0 426 20232 5

CONTENTS

Prologue

Evil cannot be tasted, seen, or touched. Yet in Killingworth, a mining community in the north east of the British Isles, the perception of evil was so overwhelming that even the fabric of the modest terraced dwellings seemed saturated with it.

Famine, earthquake and plague would all sink into insignificance if the contamination afflicting the area were not contained. Like a virus, evil would spread; national barriers, mountain ranges and oceans would be unable to offer protection. If allowed to flourish, the poisonous epidemic could reduce humankind to a harrowing role that would give a dung beetle superior status . . .

1

House of Evil

In a swirl of dust, a small avalanche of coal was being tipped from a truck on an overhead track. Simultaneously a bell pealed, clangorously signalling the end of a shift. Flexing his shoulders, the begrimed miner manning the tipping operation, straightened, easing his aching spine. No sophisticated machinery existed to lighten his burden. No lifts or mechanical loaders. No pithead showers or automated equipment. For this was England at the beginning of the nineteenth century, prior to the age of the machine.

As the miner, Jack Ward, descended from the track, he was joined by others coming off shift. Dirty, dragging weary feet, they made for the tavern to wash the coal dust from their throats before trudging the muddy roads to the tiny, stone-built cottages that were their homes.

But Jack Ward did not enter the tavern.

'Not coming in, Jack?' Tim Bass, the creases in his jovial features lined black, blinked with astonishment.

'Nay, lad, don't think I've strength to lift a Toby.'

Jack's two mates, Edwin Green and Sam Rudge, fell into step beside him. He gave them a tired grin of greeting.

'I were thinking of trying bath house!'

Rudge and Green exchanged quizzical looks. They had never been to the bath house. It was an innovation; an idea an old woman started in a derelict building not far from the pit.

'Costs though.' Sam Rudge was always money conscious. They all were, come to that; had to be.

'Aye. T'will. Even so. Just this once.' Fatal words. For as the brawny, round-faced Jack led his two friends up the hill towards the bath house, he little knew that he was leading them into a macabre and horrendous trap that would completely change their lives . . .

Little did the Doctor know of the trap he was heading for either.

The TARDIS was performing impeccably. Not an unknown phenomenon. In fact, just what was expected from a time-machine —by the Doctor anyway. So far, no aberrations. He didn't want there to be. His young companion was excited about this trip.

Peri had expressed a wish to see Kew Gardens at the beginning of the nineteenth century, when the horti-cultural extravaganza was in its infancy. The Doctor, never loath to visit his favourite planet and curious to see the reactions of this twentieth-century botanist to the endeavours of her British forebears, was checking the console. He had set the time and space co-ordinates so that they would arrive beneath the famous lilac trees on a Royal Open Day.

'Must get the co-ordinates spot on,' he mused. 'Don't want to land the wrong side of the English Channel. Smack in Napoleon's lap!' A pause for thought. The prospect had some appeal. The Doctor placed an arm across his chest, tucking the hand under his lapel—a typical Napoleonic stance.

'Wonder why he always posed like this? Could ask him.' He rumpled his unruly mop of fair curls. 'Be infinitely more interesting than traipsing round a lot of greenhouses!'

Before he could yield to temptation, Peri came sashaying into the control room, her trim young figure decked in a becoming ankle-length gown. Yellow with red trimmings, it had shoes and parasol to match. Her dark, shiny hair, usually worn short and straight, was fashioned into a bun with bobbing ringlets. She looked good and felt good.

'Hey, Doctor, this is great.'

'The costume is too large?' His mind was still with Napoleon.

'Large?' She was puzzled. The fit was perfect.

'Isn't that a synonym for "great"?'

Anticipating an inevitable lecture on the purity of the language, Peri pirouetted towards him. She wasn't about to get into an argument. Any minute now – given nothing went wrong with the temperamental TARDIS – she'd be in Kew Gardens. Mixing with royalty! The Doctor seemed a big hit wherever he appeared, so maybe she'd get an audience with King George the Third and his Queen! Great! Reflected glory, sure, but some honour for her, just plain Perpugilliam Brown of New England, USA.

The Doctor was still artlessly absorbed in his theme. 'Of course, "great" can also be used for high degree of magnitude. Someone elevated to supremacy. Like Napoleon –!'

A judder!

A tremendous lurch!

Taken by surprise, the Doctor and Peri were thrown off balance. He clung to the console, but she, in the midst of a graceful pirouette, was sent reeling . . .

The old crone running the bath house squinted myopically at the approaching miners. She was swathed in a voluminous, coarse, grey dress that brushed the cobblestones. A shawl, draped over her straggly tresses, practically concealed her gnarled and wizened features.

'Tha's the wise ones. First here, when water's hot and clean.' She extended a mittened hand for payment.

'Nay, not wise, Granma. Just fair wore out.' Jack gave her a coin, little dreaming that his hard-earned

11

cash was about to buy him the worst experience of his life . . .

A final tremendous shudder then the TARDIS settled onto an even keel.

'What is it? What's happening?' Despite her frequent exposure to the machine's eccentricities, Peri was scared. Already at battle-stations, the Doctor scrutinised the stabilising unit.

'Well?' Peri's anxiety made her sound aggressive.

'I've never felt better.' The Doctor's quip was not what she wanted to hear, right now.

'Mm. Cracks like that tell me just one thing!'

'What?' Concentrating on the display, the Doctor was patently equivocating.

'Frankly, that you haven't a clue what's going on!'

She was wrong. The Doctor did know what was going on. The TARDIS was being manoeuvred off course. At least, not entirely off course. Closer study of the panel showed that the date co-ordinates remained the same. It was the location that had been changed.

'Been changed?' responded Peri when he explained. 'Who by?'

'Whom!' The Doctor jabbed at the controls, trying to persuade the locator back to the setting for Kew. 'To use your vernacular, Peri, I haven't a clue!'

Not absolutely true. He had. They were suffering a navigational distortion; from a source situated on Earth.

'Well – well, er – what could cause a navigational distortion? Don't you know?'

'A very potent force. Equal to that of the TARDIS. Another time-machine, maybe.'

A time-machine? Overriding their controls? Pulling them off course? Why? Questions tumbled over each other in Peri's mind. Her response though, when it came, had some merit.

12

'I don't quite get it, Doctor. I mean – if this is caused by a time-machine, then someone has to be operating it.'

'Logical.'

'Then who? Not the Daleks! Surely not them!'

'Possible, but reason tells me not probable.'

'A distress call?'

'Could be.' He promptly torpedoed her relief. 'If so, why not communicate with us?'

'Insufficient power?'

'There was enough to neutralise our time and space continuum.'

Which, for Peri, meant the abduction was not benign. This was no congenial invitation. They were being shanghaied.

Exactly what the Doctor was thinking.

The old crone ushered the fatigued miners into the bath chamber. Formerly two rooms of a village house, the makeshift chamber's only furniture consisted of four wooden hip baths.

As Jack Wood tested the inviting warm water, he pulled off his neckerchief and tossed it towards a hook. It missed and fell.

'Oh, stay there. I've hardly energy to wash, let alone bend to pick thee up!'

The slim-built Edwin Green, although just as weary, reclaimed the sweat-soiled neckerchief and hung it on the hook. Jack mustered a smile of thanks for his friend.

Discarding his frayed, hopsack jacket, the brawny Sam Rudge worried about the money he had wasted. 'Wasted? It would save missus hauling tin bath into kitchen. Save stoking t'fire to heat water.' In summer he could dowse himself under the pump in the yard. But this was not summer and the only warmth in Sam's scanty cottage was from an all-purpose grate where his wife baked the bread and cooked the stews that formed the mainstay of their diet. 'Wasted? Nay, t'were money well spent.'

Was it?

None of them noticed a small pipe in the corner . . . or the jet of crimson steam infiltrating the atmosphere . . .

'Eh, this feels grand!' Green, clothes dumped in a jumble on a reed mat, was immersing himself in the soothing water.

The jet puffed into a fluffy cloud.

'Hey up! What's this? Fireworks?' said Rudge, stifling a yawn.

'Well, 'tis not smoke from fire, I'll tell thee that.'

'Dost know where's coming from, Jack?' Green, dripping suds, clambered out of the bath.

'Pipe in't corner, looks like.'

''appen us could stuff it up.'

'Aye.' Rolling a sock into a ball, Rudge plunged into a crimson mist. 'Best call old woman. 'Tis her –'

A strangled sigh.

'Can't breathe –' He slumped to the floor.

'Sam!'

Before the dumbfounded Ward and Green could render assistance to their friend, the spreading cloud enveloped them. Lungs polluted, they succumbed to the contaminating steam.

But the miners' ordeal had only just begun.

A crack appeared in the solid granite wall . . . widened . . . the halves separated . . . and glided apart.

Poised in the gap were two bizarre shapes. Muscular humans, their heads were encased in begoggled alloy masks with serpentine nozzled filters.

In automated accord, they converged on Jack Ward and carried him into the secret cavity . . .

2

The Scarecrow

'Some substitute for Kew Gardens!'

Peri's disgust was justified. The TARDIS had materialised at the foot of a slag heap.

A slag heap!

She eyed the mountain of waste from a coalmine with displeasure as the black sludge stained her new red shoes.

'Try looking on the bright side.' Endeavouring to be conciliatory, the Doctor was nevertheless concentrating on a hand-sized, oblong meter he held. 'After all, isn't coal fossilized plant life?' He was methodically sweeping all points of the compass with the device.

'What've you got there?' Curiosity overcame disappointment.

'Tracking device. Nifty gadget. Unique. Invented it myself.'

'That I can believe!'

'Registers time distortion. Should indicate the source of the power that interfered with our co-ordinates – aaaaah!' The gadget began bleeping. Obviously this was the signal the Doctor had been seeking. 'Hoist up your skirts, Peri, we're off!'

Holding the bleeping tracking device aloft, he sloshed through the slurry.

Aware that every step was making her shoes even messier, Peri trailed reluctantly in his wake.

There was no mess or dirt on Jack Ward, Edwin Green or Sam Rudge. Nor were they unconscious any longer.

The cloud of steam had evaporated and the wall was restored to normal.

Indeed, the bath chamber was just as it had been when they first entered: the baths, the fireplace, the rush mats on the floor. Nothing had changed . . . except the men themselves.

The tiredness had disappeared. So had the friendship. They were fighting. Boisterous. Hyperactive. Flicking each other with towels.

A particularly vicious swipe stung Edwin Green. He raised his fists, sparring up to Rudge. Only too willing to join combat, Rudge accepted the challenge. The fight was no horseplay. The blows drew blood.

Bored with their antics, Jack Ward elbowed them out of his way and made for the door. Glaring pugnaciously, irritably, he chafed a sore place on the left side of his neck where a round, crimson mark now glowed . . .

Separated by his aggressive departure, Ward and Green abandoned their fight and followed after him. They, too, were rubbing their necks.

On the left side.

Where similar round, crimson marks glowed . . .

Outside the bath house, completely unaware that anything alien had happened to them, their aggression focused on a crippled street-vendor who was selling a bag of muffins to a boy.

With a snarl of rage, Green booted the boy aside, Ward knocked the vendor to the ground and Rudge upended the serving tray.

Incited by the havoc they had created, kicking the scattered muffins, they stormed through the village, whooping and yelling.

It was unnaturally quiet in the field where Peri and the Doctor walked. Not that Peri had registered this. She was studying the hedgerows.

'Most of these hedgerows won't exist soon,' she said.

16

Neither Peri nor the tracking device occupied the Doctor. The finely tuned sixth sense that every Time Lord has was troubling him.

'In the twentieth century, I mean. They're being chopped down to improve farming efficiency,' Peri continued.

Again no reply from the Doctor whose unease was increasing. Whatever was unsettling him had a familiar and disagreeable echo.

'My generation's already worried about the effect on wildlife. Some species of butterfly are almost extinct. Birds too.'

'Talking of birds – have you noticed anything strange?'

Peri resisted the obvious retort that everything about and connected with the Doctor was strange. 'Strange?'

'No birdsong . . . and no birds.'

Becoming conscious of the eerie silence, she pointed to a scarecrow mounted on a frame in mid-field. 'Could be the scarecrow.'

'They're not usually this effective.' Would a solitary, straw-filled effigy so frighten the birds that none of them dared come near?

Peri broke into his thoughts. 'Well, if the place gives you the creeps, let's get out of it!' She strode to a gate giving onto a copse. The Doctor tagged behind, still vaguely perturbed.

Had he glanced back he would have had even more reason to feel perturbed. The scarecrow's inclined head, in its floppy-brimmed hat, slowly began to lift . . .

Hungry for strife, Jack Ward and his aggressive cohorts checked their rowdy progress along a leafy country lane.

Coming towards them, at a steady trot, was a horse drawn dray. The drayman recognised Jack.

'Finished for t'day, Jack?'

Jack did not respond. Instead, three abreast, the men formed a solid barrier.

Ignorant of the degeneration that had transformed the miners, the drayman chivvied them. 'Come on, lads. Out of road. Got to deliver this lot to pit!' This 'lot' was a crateload of machinery.

His words fell on deaf ears. Jack Ward unsheathed a thin, razor-sharp knife.

Disquieted, the drayman cracked his whip, an action that met with unflinching contempt from Rudge, who grabbed the snapping thong and yanked the drayman from his seat. Recklessly indifferent to the neighing, rearing horse, Ward severed the lead rein before joining in the attack – but not on the drayman. The target was the cargo. With unbridled fury, the three assailants levered the crate from the dray, sending it crashing to the ground.

Recovering, wielding a shovel, the drayman entered the fray and thwacked Jack Ward, knocking him out. Reprisal came immediately; a savage blow from Green felled him.

The ungovernable aggression continued unabated, venting its fury upon the heavy machinery; reducing the thick cast-iron mouldings to unusable fragments.

The distant hubbub of splintering metal and the terrified neighing of the horse shattered the peace of the copse. The Doctor's pace quickened as he hastened towards a stile.

Vandalism completed, without bothering to check whether their wounded comrade was alive or dead, the elated Ward and Green decamped. They passed the stile fractionally before the Doctor vaulted the crossbar.

He hurried to the horse, soothing and calming it.

'Ow-w-ch!' The groan came from beneath the jumble of broken timber and packing straw. Extricating him-

18

self from the debris, the drayman sagged to his knees.

'Here, let me help.' Peri's well-meant offer earned a rebuke.

'No, don't move him.' The Doctor's swift but adept examination showed the man's injuries to be superficial.

'They'd got no cause to behave like that,' he complained.

'Why did they attack you?' Peri's question was addressed to the drayman but the Doctor answered.

'They didn't. They attacked the machinery.'

'That's right, Miss. That's what they was after.'

'I'm lost. Why would anyone want to smash machinery?'

'They're scared it'll rob them of their jobs.' That was the drayman's explanation. The Doctor failed to agree.

'You suspect another motive, Doctor?'

'Let's say I'm keeping an open mind.'

Before Peri could query the ambiguity of this remark, they heard a moan from the ditch.

'Jack Ward. I clouted him wi' shovel.'

Avoiding a tuft of stinging nettles, the Doctor clambered into the ditch.

'Odd that,' the drayman continued to Peri. 'Leaving him behind. The three of them's always been such mates.'

The Doctor, too, had found something odd – the crimson mark on Ward's neck.

'Unusual sort of mark. Any idea how you got it –'

A belligerent shove sent the Doctor sprawling. Then, flourishing a piece of timber from the broken crate, Ward rose and began backing away.

'Steady now. Only trying to help.' The Doctor's reassurance was futile. Having gained several metres, Ward turned and hared off.

'So much for playing the Good Samaritan!' Peri quipped.

'Don't know what's got into him. Can't fathom it.

Never seen him like this afore.' The drayman indicated the demolished machinery. 'Mister Stephenson's not going to be well pleased when he sees this!'

'Stephenson?' the Doctor asked.

The drayman nodded. 'Waiting for them parts, he is.'

'George Stephenson?'

'Aye, sir. Dost know him?'

'Know of him. Peri, how d'you like to meet a genius?'

She could not resist. 'I thought I already had!'

'No, Peri. I've never changed the course of history. Indeed, I'm forbidden to do so. But George Stephenson will!'

Suddenly serious, Peri ventured a thought. 'Could that be what this is all about?'

'An astute observation.'

This was not sarcastic; the compliment was sincere. George Stephenson was important. His impact on earth's development was fundamental. He invented the railway train. Indeed, without the train, it is doubtful that Peri's own country, the United States of America, would have become one nation.

Then, with a customary, infuriating switch of mood, the Doctor decided he must meet the inventor.

'Can you give us a lift?'

To Peri's chagrin, the drayman was willing to oblige.

'Dare I question your sense of priorities?' she asked.

'You've done so before. Hop aboard!'

If the Time Lord had been concentrating less on George Stephenson, he might have noticed a weird apparition at the stile.

As the clip-clop of the horse's hoofs began, the ragged scarecrow, exuding a pernicious aura of evil, climbed the stile to follow the dray.

3

The Old Crone

Hobbling from the bath house, the old crone beckoned to a boy booting a muffin along the gutter.

'Here! Run to tavern. Tell men who want bath to come right now!' He accepted the proffered coin. 'Warn them us won't be keeping water hot much longer,' she called.

Lingering to welcome the next batch of customers, she was startled by a high frequency bleeping from a dray rumbling past.

The electronic discord came from the Doctor's tracking device. Hanging on as the wheels jolted over the cobbled street of the village, the Doctor and Peri stared as the broadcasting bleeps grew more shrill.

'Doctor!' Peri muffled her ears and the dappled horse whinnied and shied. Frantically, the Doctor tried to subdue his errant invention and the drayman to subdue his bucking horse. Both succeeded.

'Was that significant? Or just a hiccup?'

The Doctor was not sure. They had hit a nasty bump as they reached the bath house; that could have destabilised the delicate mechanism.

Something, too, had profoundly disturbed the old crone. Suspiciously, she watched the dray clatter out of sight.

'Whoa, Daisy! Whoa!' The drayman tugged on the reins.

Coming from the tavern, Tim Bass gave a weary but friendly nod. He was accompanied by the old crone's messenger boy and two mates.

'Why are we stopping here?' The tavern had no attraction for the Doctor.

'I still feel a bit shook up. Need a Toby afore I tell them at pit about attack.'

The Doctor disembarked. 'Where will I find George Stephenson?'

'In't pit.' Nervous, taking the opportunity of using this oddly garbed but apparently benevolent individual to plead his cause, the drayman begged a favour. ''Appen tha'd put in word for me. They'll be none too pleased. 'Bout machinery.'

'Yes, yes.' Impatient to be on his way, the Doctor left the drayman to assist Peri down.

'In't mighty hurry, isn't he, Miss? Dost mean summat's wrong? More than attack on machinery?'

'It does, I'm afraid. But don't ask me what.'

Nothing seemed to be wrong at the bath house as the tired but cheery Tim Bass, a scarf jauntily wound about his forehead, paid the old crone.

'We're not last, Granma. T'others'll be along when t'emptied Tobys.'

Ushering the three miners inside, she looked again in the direction the dray took . . . then peered along the street in the opposite direction. A moment's consideration . . . before following Tim Bass in.

What was she looking for? And why? The expression on her wrinkled face boded more than idle curiosity.

The answer did not come until the door slammed firmly shut. A floppy-brimmed hat was cast onto the mud. Wisps of discarded straw floated on the breeze. From the shelter of an adjacent alley came the scarecrow. Gone were the ragged labourer's jacket, tattered trousers and dirt-stained shirt. Now he wore a black velvet frock-coat with a silver encrusted collar and velvet trousers to match. His hair was carefully combed, his black beard and moustache elegantly trimmed. For this was the Master, the Doctor's implacable enemy.

Fastidiously brushing the last vestiges of chaff from his sleeve, he gazed at the bath house. A sardonic smile stretched his lips at the sound of the bolt being thrust home.

'Primitive. An insult.' The smile faded. 'But first things first. I've a death to arrange.' He strode purposefully off in pursuit of the Doctor.

'What've they got in there? Coal, or diamonds?' Peri's remark was justified. A guard, flintlock pistol tucked in his belt, was at the pit entrance. Straining at the leash, fangs bared, his dog snarled a challenge to all intruders.

'Machinery, Peri. More specifically, George Stephenson. And he's –'

'You told me. One of the architects of the Industrial Revolution.'

'And I didn't exaggerate. Without his genius, your precious twentieth century would be a much sorrier place.'

The pit gave the impression of being a fortress protected by strategically positioned armed sentries.

'We have to get past, Peri.'

'Easier said . . . That dog doesn't look as though it's been fed today!'

In typical fashion, deciding to brazen his way in, and giving his pink lapel a confident tug, the Doctor strutted forward.

'Oy! Where dost think tha's going?' The guard lengthened the leash and the dog leapt ferociously, jaws snapping.

'To see George Stephenson. Can you tell me where he'll be?'

The Doctor's bluff cut no ice with the guard. It would be jeopardising his job to disobey orders. And there could be little doubt what they were!

'No-one gets in here without a pass.'

'My dear man, a pass? I am a VIP.' Autocratic as ever. But useless.

'If tha be here for t'meeting, tha'd have special pass.'

Meeting? The Doctor's curiosity was aroused. What meeting could the man be blathering about?

Resignedly accepting that once launched on a course of action the Doctor was unstoppable, Peri adopted the role of mediator. 'We've been travelling. The pass obviously never reached us.'

The guard remained obdurate. 'Then tha's name will be on't list.' He consulted a clipboard which the Doctor instantly commandeered.

'James Watt, Thomas Telford, Michael Faraday, Humphrey Davy,' he read aloud. 'Good heavens, Peri, d'you recognise these names?'

Peri did. She'd learned about them in school. All of them. This was a period in England when genius seemed to bloom. 'I'm not totally illiterate! What's the noun for a collection of geniuses? A bevy?'

'An inspiration, perhaps? I don't know. But I do know the men who will be at this meeting transformed history.'

The guard had had enough of their nonsense. He snatched the sheet. 'Is tha name on't list?'

'An oversight.'

'Oh, aye. A genius too, art tha?'

'Indeed I am.' Modesty was not one of the Doctor's virtues. 'I'm also an inventor.' He waggled the tracer under the guard's nose. The dog growled.

More afraid of the slavering fangs than of the Doctor's disapproval, Peri took over. 'I must apologise.' A winsome smile. She'd always been told she had an attractive smile. 'The Doctor's a little eccentric.'

Attractive it certainly was. The guard relented. 'Doctor, is he? I could maybe ask in't office.'

'Would you? How kind.' Another bewitching smile.

'Harry!' His deputy came from the hut. 'The gate. Best lock it!' He shortened the dog's lead. 'This way, Miss.'

'Eccentric? Me? Preposterous!' Chuntering indignantly, the Doctor followed obediently.

The remark amused Harry. Nevertheless, he, too, exercised obedience and secured the gate.

In doing so, he flirted with death.

The contretemps between the Doctor and the guard had permitted the Master to catch up. Now the locking of the gate was preventing him from entering. He toyed with the TCE – his unique and deadly Tissue Compression Eliminator. A short blast and this paltry minion would be despatched to oblivion.

Luckily for Harry, the renegade Time Lord was not ready to reveal his presence. Angrily changing tack, he prowled the perimeter fence seeking an alternative way in.

A winning smile from a petite young lady might have enchanted the guard, but it had not beguiled him. He escorted Peri and the Doctor into the unoccupied office.

Furnished with a polished mahogany desk and an Windsor chair, this was manifestly the domain of an important personage. A glass-fronted bookcase housed a modest library of leather-bound volumes. Fluted oil-lamps completed the decor.

'If tha'll sit thee down, I'll see if I can find Mister Stephenson.'

'I'll come with you –'

'Nay. Tha'll bide here wi' young lady.' He unhooked the leash. 'Stay!'

With the guard's departure, the ferocious hound crouched vigilantly on the threshold.

'Good dog. Good Fido.' The Doctor immediately tried to sidle past. 'Good boy, then. Let the nice Doctor through.'

His reward was a menacing growl.

'I guess he's not susceptible to your irresistible charm!' jibed Peri.

'Occasionally – just occasionally – your smugness infuriates me!'

Reacting to his tone the dog's growl grew more intimidating.

'Keep your voice down!' said Peri. 'Time Lords may not get rabies, but humans do! And that dog looks more than ready to bite!'

'Will you stop prattling about the dog!' The Doctor's tetchiness was not just due to Peri's smugness. 'Something's going on here. I don't fully understand what.' He raised the lace curtain and rattled the window. 'But I'm increasingly convinced it's got to be stopped!'

'Could be you're jumping the gun.'

'Really? That's your assessment?' He abandoned the window. 'Did you see the date at the top of that list? In less than two days, a meeting will take place – here – of the greatest practical talents the human race has ever produced. A coincidence?'

'Unlikely, I agree.'

'Well, hanging about in an office isn't going to provide the answer!'

Snarling, ears pricked, the dog rose on its haunches. Convinced that at any moment the aroused animal would attack, Peri retreated to the Doctor's side. 'I warned you to cool it!'

'It's not me.'

The dog bared its fangs and sprang.

But not at them. Instead it leapt from the office, yelping and howling.

'Doctor – that dog's really spooked. I wonder why?'

Sprinting between the sheds, the dog raced for the pit

gate. Once there, it threw itself at the bars in a desire to maul the black velvet-clad figure tampering with the padlock. Having failed in his quest for an alternative access, the Master had returned.

In a bedlam of barking, almost demented, the animal repeatedly hurled itself against the gate.

Silencing the brute was easy. A single burst from the TCE, a pathetic whine, and then one dog less in the Universe . . .

But succumbing to his callous impulse had brought the Master a further difficulty. Attracted by the din, emerging from the hut, Harry had witnessed the slaughter.

After ensuring there were no other observers, the Master levelled the TCE again. The petal-shaped segments of the bulbous nozzle separated and a searing white light homed in on its target.

Harry's luck had run out after all.

4

Death Fall

'It's stopped!'

The Doctor, having vacated the office, was again using his tracking device to locate the power that had re-routed the TARDIS. Misinterpreting Peri's remark, he rapped the tracer. 'No, it's still functioning.'

'The dog! It's not barking!'

The Doctor paused, listening, suddenly very solemn. ' "There was silence deep as death".'

'That's morbid.'

'Possibly.'

The grim quotation merely vocalised the overwhelming foreboding of evil that plagued him; an evil so tangible, he felt the source must be close by.

Showing no remorse, the Master was again examining the gate padlock when the shattering of glass interrupted him. Indiscriminately, Ward and his fellow aggressors were wreaking havoc upon the village street. Ever the opportunist, he decided to recruit them.

'You there!' His curt command halted them. 'You were in the lane, smashing machinery.'

'Never mind machinery. What's tha' doing here?' Ward was in no mood to be treated as a subordinate.

'That's easy. He's one of brainy ones on't list. Arrived here early for this scurvy meeting.' For Rudge, the world was infested with enemies.

'Aye, come to rob us of us jobs!'

'Hold hard. I intend you no harm.'

'Talks funny, don't he?' Green mimicked the

29

Master. ' "Hold hard".' He scooped up a stone. 'This hard enough?'

'Imbeciles! Are you incapable of using your brains? What advantage will attacking me bring you?'

The stone was heavy in Green's fist. The urge to aim was strong.

'You let the man you should have destroyed go free!' The Master's compelling personality as much as his rhetoric, inhibited even their uncontrollable aggression.

Ward, rubbing the crimson mark on his neck, took the accusation personally. 'I did? Let who go free? What's tha' on about?'

'In the lane. He pretended to help you. Help! He's a crony of Stephenson's. An inventor, here to mechanise the mine.'

'Dost know what he's getting at, Jack?' Rudge certainly did not.

'Doing nowt but trying to save his skin!' Jack was ready to crack his knuckles on the stranger's superior chin!

'Ask him. Ask him why he's trying to take the bread from your mouths.' The Master's contempt for these ignorant mortals was barely disguised; but he needed them. He had worked out a plan and these morons were to be part of it. They were to be used to get rid of that scourge of the Universe, the Doctor.

'Us'll do more than ask! Where is he? Dost know?'

'He's just gone into the pit.'

Inflamed by his lies, the wiry Green battered the padlock.

'Let me.' The Master intervened; the pandemonium might bring opposition. He wanted their entrance to go unannounced.

Shielding his actions from his dupes, he produced a pencil laser, talking all the while to divert them. 'You can't miss him.' A thin laser beam lanced the padlock.

'Mean looking. Wearing yellow trousers, a multi-coloured coat and a vulgar plaid waistcoat.' The description was for Rudge's and Green's benefit. Ward had already been subjected to the Doctor's sartorial splendour!

The padlock melted. He swung the gates wide and the three miners swarmed through.

'A word of warning. Go carefully. He's treacherous.'

'Careful, Peri! Careful!'

Keeping pace with the impatient Doctor, Peri had stumbled, knocking over a safety lamp as they skirted the pit shaft. 'A Davy lamp, isn't it?'

'No. A prototype. Stephenson's got a couple of years' work to do on it yet.' The discourse came absently as he swept the tracking device in an arc. 'But you're correct. Davy gets the credit. Controversial decision, I've always thought. Which reminds me – where is Stephenson?'

'He could be anywhere in this place. Even underground!' Gulping, she peered over the rim of a shaft. Seemingly stretching to infinity, the bottom could not be seen. The giddy drop induced her to sway, experience vertigo, feel as though she were about to be plucked into its inky depths . . .

A hand clutched her shoulder.

'Peri, you have an extraordinary capacity for seeking out danger.' The Doctor's words were lost on Peri. She was staring beyond him to where the miners were advancing.

'Doctor!'

Imperturbably, he lectured on. 'You must learn to avoid getting into situations –'

'*Doctor!*'

Too late. A lump of coal came whistling past his ear. Intuitively, he bundled Peri behind a truck. A random missile? Or was it meant for him? The introspective

31

debate was rudely terminated. With arrogant ease, the brawny Ward sent the truck trundling along the track and the three vengeful aggressors closed in.

'Peri! Get away from here!'

'But –'

'Don't argue! Go!' His concern for Peri made him unwary. His toe stubbed against a rail causing him to stagger. A smart punch from Green jerked the tracer from his grip, lobbing it over the edge of the shaft. After what appeared to be an eternity, there came a faint thud.

'Now you really have gone too far! The effort that went into constructing –'

A man of deeds rather than chitchat, Rudge lunged at the Doctor. A crash barrier might have averted disaster. But this was the nineteenth century and there was none. Briefly, they tottered on the brink . . . then fell . . .

The Doctor grabbed for the lift rope.

So did Rudge.

The Doctor succeeded. Not so Rudge.

His protracted, diminishing scream underscored the sickening drop to the bottom.

Incensed by the fate of his companion, Green snatched up a pit prop and, with frenetic fury, stabbed at the Doctor, trying to force him to lose his tenuous hold on the rope.

Releasing one hand, the Doctor reached for the edge of the shaft to steady his dangling body. A spade, wielded by Ward, chopped at the straining fingers . . . missing by a hair's breadth as the Doctor snatched them away.

He clung desperately onto the rope. But his weight and the constant blows were beginning to tell. Resourcefulness was basic to his nature, yet even that had deserted him. Could it be that escape was impossible? Ridiculous though it seemed, he wondered if falling to one's death was the same as drowning. Would all his previous lives flash before him? The drop was long enough!

'Get away from him!' Peri had not capitulated. 'Leave him alone!'

She pelted chunks of coal at Ward and Green. A hit and miss affair. Some found their targets, some found the beleagured Doctor.

'Help! Please help! They're crazy! They'll kill him!'

If her aim was erratic, her predictions were perilously near to being accurate; the Doctor's stamina was fast ebbing away.

Spurred on by his weakening grasp, the antagonists thrust with increasing fervour.

Bang!

A burst of gunfire!

'Stop that or I'll blast you to Kingdom come!'

There was no disputing that the warning was genuine. Nor was there any doubting the authority in the voice. The attackers scarpered.

The man behind the blunderbuss had not finished giving orders. 'Quickly! Haul that fellow to safety!'

The guard who had accompanied Peri and the Doctor to the office sprang to carry out the command. It had come from his boss, Lord Ravensworth, the mine owner.

Restored to terra firma, the Doctor could not resist a quip. 'Almost at the end of my tether, eh?'

'It's no joke, Doctor!'

An opinion shared by Lord Ravensworth as he rejected the Doctor's expressions of gratitude. 'Perhaps you'll tell me who you are. And I don't want any flummery about VIPs. I'm Lord Ravensworth, the owner. I issued – personally – the invitations to the meeting. And your face is not one I recall!' Nor was this bombast; his lordship was plainly not to be trifled with. 'VIP's indeed!' A peremptory gesture. 'My office!'

Reaching the office, a chastened Doctor was apologetic. 'We shouldn't have deceived the guard. But how else could we have got into the mine?'

'Spare me the dubious pragmatism. Came to see George Stephenson, you say?'

'I'm a great admirer.'

Ravensworth was sceptical. 'Must be if you're pre- pared to resort to trickery! How do I know you're not in league with these machinery wreckers? These wretched Luddites?'

'Luddites' was the name given to groups of artisans who were rioting and smashing machinery throughout the industrial centres of England; workers who feared the new-fangled contraptions were going to deprive them of their livelihoods.

'Really! Do I look like a man who would wreck machines?'

Wincing, Peri offered up a silent prayer at this hostage to fortune!

Sourly, Ravensworth eyed the Doctor's flamboyant attire. Abruptly, he took the Doctor's hands and in- spected the palms. 'Certainly you've never done a day's labour in your life!' Disregarding the Doctor's affronted look, he continued. 'It's possible you may even be a gentleman.'

Although sharing his employer's doubts about the interloper's status, the guard had other worries. 'Shall us get searching for them two who attacked this – er – gentleman, m'lord?'

'Leave them. They'll have gone to ground.'

'Leave them!' Peri was indignant. 'They wanted to kill the Doctor!'

'I'm not disputing that, young woman. A brutal attack . . . Over thirty years Jack Ward's worked for me. In all that while I've never seen him raise his fist to another man.'

'Well, he's undergone a change now!'

The brittle exchange had been used by the Doctor to assess the mine owner. Could the tall, elegant aristocrat be a party to whatever was affecting this area? Were the paramilitary security arrangements there as a deterrent? Or were they protecting a secret?

'The disruptions only started recently?'

The fine-boned features framed in grey whiskers, puckered with concern. 'Disruption's a tardy description.' He lifted the tail of his brown frock-coat as he sat on the Windsor chair. 'There've been Luddite riots all over the country. But here . . .' He shrugged.

'It's been more extreme?' The Doctor finished the sentence.

'The violence has been atrocious!'

'Murderous would be more apt!'

'Peri!' The Doctor's reproval was sharp.

'No, the young lady's right. I don't understand what's going on. I've always had an excellent relationship with the men. Flattered myself I enjoyed their trust and respect. Now this nightmare . . .'

'It's just the men who are affected?'

Lord Ravensworth nodded. 'Yes. Just the men. They become savage. Go berserk. Seem to suffer an utter change of personality.'

Even as he spoke, in the bath house, happy-go-lucky Tim Bass was undergoing the sinister process which would change him too . . .

5

Enter the Rani

A cleaved skull was illustrated on a computer screen. Encased in the skeleton's ivory shell, the bisected brain was depicted in sickly shades of saffron. Like a pulsating caterpillar, a catheter tube snaked from the computer to Tim Bass.

Comatose, he was lying full stretch on a trolley. The tube was clamped to the left side of his neck. A separate link led to a crystal flagon into which dripped miniscule globules of fluid. On an indentical trolley, his brain already plundered, lay another miner.

The muscular humans in their serpentine masks, had carried the victims through from the bath chamber after the crimson steam had rendered them unconscious. This sophisticated laboratory was the secret cavity beyond the mysterious wall.

A note of incongruity in the clinical setting was the room divider-cum-mural. The volcanic picture, painted in fiery-oranges and scarlets, formed a paradoxical backing to the two muscular humans positioned before it. The masks now fastened at their waists, they stared unseeingly into space; mortal robots, programmed and waiting.

'Take him through. Bring the other one!'

Activated, moving in unison, they lifted the miner from the trolley.

But who had spoken?

Surely not the rheumaticky old crone. The voice was vigorous and firm. Yet it was she hunched over the keyboard. The cursor began a steady decline. An irascible huff as she realigned Tim's extractor clamp.

The huff would have expressed more than irascibility had the old crone known who was spying on the activity of her human slaves in the chamber.

With the Doctor temporarily out of his malignant reach, the Master was exploring fresh avenues of mischief. Using his electronic magnet, he had slid the door bolt from its socket and stolen into the bath house. Intrigued, he watched as the muscular humans humped the next donor through the parted wall.

Unaware of the intruder, the old crone was meticulously pouring a meagre amount of fluid into a phial. Sealing the phial, she glanced at the now empty flagon . . . reflected in the crystal surface was the Master's mocking smile.

'No welcome?'

'You're not!' Her hostility was unequivocal.

'Fascinating!' The Master surveyed the laboratory and all its intricate apparatus. 'But then, anything connected with you would undoubtedly be fascinating, my dear Rani.'

Rani? He knew her? This withered old crone?

Old crone? The shoulders were no longer hunched. The infirm spine was erect. And as the shawl slipped from her head, she ripped off the latex facial disguise to reveal the unblemished skin and sculptured beauty of a woman in her prime. Her most striking feature was her eyes; two glittering sapphires, they projected an icy calculation unflawed by compassion.

'I thought that last mad scheme of yours had finished you for good!'

'You jest, of course.' Conceit reverberated from every syllable. 'I am indestructible! The whole Universe knows that!'

'What happened?' Detached scientific curiosity.

'The extreme heat generated sufficient numismaton gas for me to return to my usual healthy size and self.'

'Pity.' The Rani meant it.

'Really, my dear Rani, you and I should be friends. I am one of your greatest admirers.'

'Don't bother with flattery.' She was too shrewd to be taken in by such an obvious ploy. 'I know why you're here. I saw the Doctor.' She had. When he passed on the dray and his tracer had let out its erratic bleeps.

'Then you know why I need your co-operation.'

'Co-operation! I want nothing to do with you!' She was adamant.

'You may change your mind when you hear my proposition.'

'I'm not concerned with your pathetic vendetta, one way or the other.' She checked the seal on the phial. 'Now clear off and let me get on with my work.'

Her obduracy was not unexpected, but coercion came easily to the Master. 'Either you collaborate or I bring this little venture to an extremely untimely end!' Deliberately, he jiggled Tim Bass's catheter tube, causing the skull image on the monitor screen to flutter.

'Josh! Tom! Kill!'

Her two muscular assistants reacted immediately.

But so did the Master.

A rapid blast from the TCE – and Tom disintegrated in the enveloping red haze.

Unerringly, the TCE set Josh in its sights.

'No, Josh! Stand still!'

With life-saving subservience, Josh obeyed the Rani's imperative command.

Another woman, someone quite unlike the Rani, was also interested in Josh's welfare. Cradling their baby son in her arms, Josh's wife had sought an appointment with Lord Ravensworth.

'My Josh, your lordship. He's been missing for days.'

'It's not just her Josh that's missing. Our Tom's gone too.' This was from an older woman. Both had come to

39

the office in the forlorn hope that the mine owner could offer an explanation.

Before he had a chance to answer, the Doctor butted in. 'When?'

Neither woman replied; his lordship's frown indicated his annoyance at the Doctor's interjection.

'Forgive me, Ravensworth. It is important.' He elaborated his question. 'When did they go missing?'

The older woman replied. 'Nowt's been seen of them since they come off shift together.'

'Perhaps they've joined those Luddites?' Peri's contribution distressed the women.

'Joined that mob of lunatics,' the older woman retorted. 'Smashing and rampaging day and night! Frightening folks out of us beds!'

The younger woman was equally vehement. 'My Josh wouldn't join them. My Josh wouldn't harm anyone. He's gentle as a lamb is my Josh.'

If she could have seen her Josh at that moment, she would not have spoken with such certainty.

Acting on the Rani's instructions, he was in the bath chamber where, unceremoniously, he rolled the still unconscious miner onto his back.

'You and the Doctor are a well matched pair of pests! Now I need a new assistant!' Directed at the Master, the Rani's ill-tempered remark confirmed that saving Josh's life had nothing to do with kindness; she simply did not want to be inconvenienced. She unscrewed the ventilated lid of a small oval container. Inside, wriggling and glowing fluorescently, was a colony of sickly-green maggots.

Selecting a plump specimen, she held it to the miner's lips and forced his mouth open. The maggot, squirming, was popped onto his tongue.

Even the Master shuddered as the miner, his Adam's Apple bobbing, chewed, then swallowed the revolting morsel.

His eyelids blinked wide.

The pupils became suffused with a blue glow. Gradually the blue faded and the eyes stared fixedly into space. Just like Josh's eyes.

The Master's admiration for the Rani soared. 'I wasn't wrong. I knew with you as controller it wouldn't be hypnotism. Not from a chemist of your calibre! What are they? Parasites you've specially impregnated?'

'There's an easy way to find out. Try some.' She offered the container with its slimy, squiggling grubs, not expecting him to accept.

He didn't. Make a selection, that is. He grabbed the lot!

Furious, she tried to retrieve them. No chance. The Master was never going to surrender such a valuable acquisition.

'Brilliant! Quite brilliant!' The tribute was sincere. 'When the Time Lords exiled you they made a cardinal error.'

'Yes. They did. And they'll learn to regret it!' There was no doubting the Rani's threat. 'So will anyone else who interferes!'

6

Miasimia Goria

'Doctor, let's get out of here! I don't just mean this office. Away from Killingworth!'

This earnest advice was not the result of thought transference; Peri had not plugged into the Rani's wavelength. She had merely applied logic; a discipline acquired and honed during her studies to be a botanist.

'You're in danger! That attack wasn't random! Those louts tried to kill you!'

Disgruntled from the protracted and fruitless cross-examination of the two miners' wives, the Doctor took the acrimonious logic a stage further. 'True. But why? Aren't you interested in why they should make me their target?'

'Not in the least. I can't think of a better reason for abandoning this visit.'

The Doctor recognised a fallacy when he heard it. 'You're forgetting. We didn't just stumble into this place. We were hijacked.'

'I'm forgetting nothing. The Luddites are not our problem.'

Maddeningly, he agreed.

The penny dropped. 'You don't believe it is the Luddites.' Not a question, an accusation.

'Do you?' he challenged.

Her silence confirmed that she, too, had reached the same conclusion.

'Until I know what's going on, we stay.' The curt declaration brooked no more argument. He prowled the office, caged by his own inadequacies. Despite his verbal dexterity, he was unable to reassemble the mosaic into a pattern that made sense.

Equally flummoxed by the irrational sequence of events, Ravensworth steered the distraught women he was escorting away from the shaft; the recent incident would only add to their anguish. Even so, the massive cogged wheel's gaunt silhouette could be glimpsed above the shed roofs. A stark reminder of the ills besetting the once tranquil hamlet.

The baby Josh's wife was nursing, whimpered. She cuddled him protectively, but the infant refused to be comforted.

''Tis his feeding hour.'

'Can I get the drayman to give you a lift?'

'Nay, m'lord. Thanks kindly.'

'Aye. Shouldn't have bothered you.' The older woman was near to tears. 'But us were that worried.'

'I'll instruct my foreman to make enquiries among those on the shift.' Ravensworth signalled the guard to open the gate. 'We'll find them.'

His composed assurance hid gnawing pangs of uncertainty as he contemplated the barricaded village street. In the best spirit of paternalism, he had given the people of his estates protection and leadership. Now he was failing them. The slough of despond deepened; a pall of smoke curled on the horizon. Ravensworth prayed it was just a hayrick and not the thatched homestead of a tenant farmer being razed. Normally he would have organised a fire-fighting party, but he could not afford to deplete the defences of the mine.

'Lord Ravensworth!'

The Doctor was calling from the pit shaft.

'Can you arrange for that poor fellow to be brought to the surface?'

'You should co-operate with me, you know,' the Master

44

told the Rani. 'The Doctor's had two run-ins with the results of your handiwork.'

She was disconnecting Tim Bass from the computer. The Master persisted. 'He won't tolerate someone deliberately playing havoc with his favourite planet.'

'Can't you get it into your warped skull that there is nothing deliberate about it! The aggression's an unfortunate side effect.'

'Unfortunate? Fortuitous would be a more apposite epithet!'

'Put it how you like. I need the chemical. The only source is the human brain.' Careful to spill none of the small amount of liquid, she began to tip it from the crystal flagon into the phial. 'It can have no relevance to you or your machinations.'

'Ah, but then, as yet you are not apprised of my purpose in being here.' He was registering the extreme caution with which she performed the task.

'To destroy the Doctor. You've never had any other. It obsesses you to the exclusion of all else.'

He was amused; did this arid, calculating chemist think his plans were that naive? 'You underestimate me. Certainly I want to destroy the Doctor. To see him suffer. But that will be an exquisite preliminary step. I have a greater concept. A concept that will encompass the whole human race!'

The Rani studied him like a specimen on a slide. 'You're unbalanced.' She resealed the phial. 'No wonder the Doctor always outwits you!'

The Master's euphoria vanished. In an angry sweep, he whipped the phial from her grasp.

It had the desired effect. 'Give that to me!' she cried.

Relishing the anxiety in her voice, he examined the contents. 'Don't get much, do you?'

'There's only a minute amount in each brain.'

Prudence tempered her response; the fluid represented all she had achieved to date; goad him, and the volatile wretch would have no compunction about spilling the lot.

'Why does extracting this make humans so aggressive?'

She remained mute. She did not want to share anything with the megalomaniac. Most of all the secrets of her research.

But the Master had the initiative. He began to tip the phial. 'I'll not ask again . . .'

Her reply was prompt. 'Because without that chemical the brain cannot rest.'

A beatific smile. 'Ah, now I understand. You need it for your aliens.'

The sharp reaction betrayed her surprise.

'On Miasimia Goria.' He was savouring her confusion. More than just pique caused the flush on her cheeks at the mention of Miasimia Goria. She had striven to keep her conquest of the planet concealed.

He could not resist needling her. 'Oh, I dropped in on your domain before following you here. Chaos! Complete mayhem! What went wrong?'

'Wrong? Who said anything went wrong?'

'You rule there. Absolutely. I assume one of your schemes didn't turn out quite as you expected.'

The Rani was defensive. 'An insignificant affair. In the process of heightening the awareness of my aliens, I lowered their ability to sleep. They became –'

'– difficult to control. On the other hand, with this . . .' – he jiggled the precious brain fluid – 'and those impregnated parasites, their talents are yours to command. Such power . . .' Intoxicating possibilities presented themselves. 'Is that a scanner?' He rapped an opaque screen on an intricate display deck.

The Rani was still smarting, 'Find out!'

Deliberately, he unsealed the phial, allowing a droplet of the fluid to teeter on the brink. It was enough. The Rani switched on the scanner. 'Who do you want?'

'The Doctor.'

'Where did you see him last?'

'At the pit.'

She pressed three tabs, setting the co-ordinates. A magenta corona outlined the circumference, bathing the screen in a rosy hue. But the image that hardened into detail was that of a sad cortège.

Stretcher borne, draped in a blanket, Rudge's corpse was being carried from the pit shaft when the Doctor halted its progress.

Deferentially, he raised the blanket to inspect the left side of Rudge's neck. Then, while the bewildered Lord Ravensworth and Peri watched nonplussed, he inspected the necks of the stretcher bearers.

'What the blazes are you doing?'

His lordship's exasperation simmered over. Peri could have told him to save his breath!

'Do you hear me? What was that all about, man?'

'Later. You said the son of one of my attackers worked here?'

The request, without a trace of rudeness, disconcerted Ravensworth. 'Yes. Yes. Luke Ward. George Stephenson's apprentice. Very capable young man. Spotted him when he was just a lad. My protégé, as it happ –'

The Doctor cut in. 'Find him for me, there's a good chap.'

The novel role of errand boy flabbergasted the peer of the realm. He glared after the receding figure in the multicoloured jacket making for his office.

'The dratted man's a positive law unto himself!'

The Master and the Rani had observed all this on the scanner.

'You see, we *do* have an allied cause,' he said to her.

'Unless you eliminate the Doctor, he'll bring this cosy operation to an end.'

She accepted the analysis. The Doctor would dig and delve until he'd solved the puzzle. She would have to get rid of him. 'Then let's get on with it!'

'My way!' The Master's tone was firm. 'We do it my way!' He intended to impose the strategy. The precious phial that she had treasured was going to ensure his domination. 'Any idea where those morons you created might be?'

She jabbed the tabs to reset the co-ordinates.

The scene changed from the pit to a dark, disused mine. Crawling along the low tunnels were Jack Ward, Edwin Green and several miners. Every now and then, with grubby knuckles, they rubbed the crimson marks that scarred their necks.

Having noted the co-ordinates and seen all he wanted, the Master abruptly strode from the laboratory into the bath chamber.

'Where are you going?' No reply. 'The brain fluid!'

'Perfectly safe.' Ostentatiously, the Master tucked the phial into his breast pocket. 'Next to my hearts. Both of them.' He disappeared into the hallway.

Extracting something from her skirt pouch, the Rani stalked furiously across the chamber. As she flounced into the hallway – a hand clapped onto her wrist. Anticipating her pursuit, the Master had diverted into an alcove.

When she made no attempt to get free, his suspicions increased. She was being uncharacteristically supine. What was she clutching? He prised her fingers apart, revealing a pill box.

'They're capsules for my lungs. The earth's damp atmosphere affects them.'

A plausible explanation.

Even so, the wily Master was sceptical. He flipped the lid. The box contained an assortment of pills.

'Do you trust anyone?'

'Yes. Myself. Capsules they may be. But don't touch them until that door closes between us!' He exited into the street.

Glowering after him, the Rani snapped shut the pill box. With his departure, her alleged need of a capsule had also gone.

A ruse? He obviously thought so. The incident demonstrated the mutual lack of faith binding the Time Lords. Hardly an auspicious beginning to the proposed alliance.

7

A Deadly Signature

Despite his objections to the Doctor's autocratic manner, Lord Ravensworth had brought Luke Ward. Or, to be more precise, he had despatched a messenger for him.

Luke could truly be called a golden boy. Tall, fair-haired, the eighteen year old exuded honesty and intelligence. It was not difficult to comprehend Ravensworth's pride in his protégé.

He had submitted to the barrage of questions with worried concern. But, as yet, none of his replies had given the Doctor a lead. His father's reported violent behaviour was completely inexplicable.

However, the Doctor persisted. 'And you're certain your father was perfectly normal this morning?'

'The lad's told you he was!' Lord Ravensworth was losing patience with the inquisition.

'I know, I know. Bear with me. The answer's probably staring me in the face and I just can't see it.'

Realising that escape from Killingworth depended on the Doctor unravelling the mystery, Peri joined in. 'When did you last talk to your father, Luke?'

'When he came off shift. He were on't way to bath house.'

'Bath house?'

'To get cleaned up.' Luke failed to understand the Doctor's evident excitement.

'Doctor, you recall when we passed the bath house –'

'Luke, can you find me an old coat and cap?' This was not really a request.

51

'Aye, in't lobby, but . . .' Luke's orders usually came from Ravensworth. His lordship gave a fatalistic shrug. 'Do as he says.'

'Doctor, when we passed the bath house, that gadget of yours –' Again Peri was interrupted.

'Reacted. Yes. Yes. I said it had been staring me in the face, didn't I? It was! Literally!' Discarding his own jacket, he accepted the soiled coat Luke had collected from the lobby.

'I guess I should, but I don't get it.'

'Glad it's not just me!' Ravensworth said fretfully.

'Those men who attacked me. They didn't look as if they'd come straight from the pit, did they?' He struggled into the coat. 'They were clean!'

As if this explained everything, he dashed from the office.

Of the baffled trio, Ravensworth was the first to give voice. 'Is he often like this?'

'Too often. Excuse me.' Peri scooted out of the door.

She did not have far to go. The Doctor was rubbing his hands on the ground and transferring the dirt to his temples.

'Would you mind telling me what's going on?'

'I'm about to follow – as you would term it – a hunch.'

'A reply that told her nothing. A sigh of resignation. 'Okay, where do I fit in?'

'You stay here where you'll be safe.'

That did it! '*Safe!* From the moment I stepped into the TARDIS I haven't been safe!'

'How do I look?' Nose, forehead, cheeks and ears were smudged with coal dust. His teeth gleamed white as he grinned at Peri.

'Like a man who could do with a bath.'

Pleased with her reply, he donned the cap with a flourish and set off.

Little did the Rani know she was about to receive yet another unwelcome visitor. She was too preoccupied. Circled by the rosy hue on the scanner, the Master could be seen exploring the eerie disused mine. Shale scrunched beneath his polished shoes. The rotting pit props supporting the uneven roof were meshed with cobwebs that adhered to his gloves.

'A rat hole,' he muttered in disgust.

'Then you should be at home!' thought his unseen observer as she realigned the contrast.

He moved cautiously . . . alert . . . listening. He had no desire to come upon the aggressive miners unawares.

The scuff of a foot on rubble from deeper within. The Master paused . . . felt for the TCE.

'I told you to wait, you cretins!' murmured the Rani. 'Wait until he's nearer. He's armed!'

The steely command revealed that the Master had underestimated the Rani. When she had plundered the miners' brains, she had also made them her vassals. Through an implant in their necks, she could communicate instructions. Her erstwhile partner was walking into an ambush.

All was quiet. He ventured on.

'*Now!*' hissed the Rani.

In sudden, simultaneous action, Jack Ward leapt from his hiding place, cutting off the rear, and Edwin Green dropped from a ledge. He landed on top of the Master, bowling him over. Before he could recover, the agile Green pounced again, locking his opponent in a grip that prevented him from using the TCE. Frantically, the Master wrestled to get free. The writhing bodies scrunched into the rough shale.

But the Rani, too, had miscalculated. Instead of succumbing swiftly, the Master was giving an able account of himself. Her all-important phial was in danger of being crushed between the combined weights. The brain fluid would be spilt!

53

Yanking a mini-transmitter from her skirt pouch, she hurriedly tapped out a code. A micro-second later, breaking from the clinch, Green clutched at his neck. Choked. Tore at the crimson mark.

To no avail.

The crimson spread . . . slowly . . . remorselessly . . . painfully strangling Green to death . . .

'The Mark of the Rani.' The Master had correctly surmised that the fatal crimson mark was the Rani's deadly signature. Her obscene ingenuity made him more determined than ever to conscript her talents.

'Is he dead?' Jack Ward broke in on his thoughts.

The Master nodded. Already he was devising a scheme to turn the situation to his own advantage. If he could persuade these homicidal idiots that the Doctor had caused their companion to die . . . 'I warned you that inventor was treacherous. I told you to get rid of him.'

Jack Ward was perplexed. 'But he's not nowhere near.'

'He doesn't have to be. He's got a machine that does his foul work for him.' Prepared for Ward's answer, he pulled out paper and pen.

'A machine?'

'I'll show you.' He began to draw on the paper.

The Rani adjusted the controls, but was unable to bring the sketch into focus. 'What's he up to now?'

A loud hammering on the street door.

'It'll be something devious and overcomplicated.' Switching off the scanner, she quit the laboratory. 'He'd get dizzy if he tried to walk a straight line!'

But in the gloom of the old mine, the Master knew exactly what he was doing. He had drawn a sketch of the Doctor's TARDIS.

'What's that?' Ward snatched the paper. 'A coffin?'

'A coffin?' The appropriate description amused the

Master. 'It's the machine that killed your friend.'

'That thing?'

'Can you offer a better explanation?'

'Nay.' Ward's inner turmoil welled into anger again. 'Nay, I can't.'

'Then be guided by me. Take that box and bury it in the deepest shaft!'

'Can't see no point in burying a box!' Ward was a practical man. 'Better to bury *him*!'

The others nodded in agreement. Not the reaction the Master wanted at all. No wonder he had such contempt for the beings on this planet! Contrary creatures! In fact, if it weren't that he would derive pleasure from seeing the Doctor butchered by these very humans he so favoured, he'd have eliminated this crew there and then! However, not quite yet . . .

'Trust me.' The voice was ingratiating. 'I give you my word. Destroying that box will divest him of all his power.'

'Where is machine? Dost know?'

'At the slag heap. Off you go. Fetch it to the pit.'

'Fetch it?' Jack wasn't having that. He was no dimwit. 'Fetch it? Nay, tha's coming with us.' He wasn't altogether sure he trusted this glib stranger. Anyway, the left side of his neck was irritating him, making him feel tetchy.

The Master, though, had his excuse ready. 'That box is only the bait. I have to return to the village to set the trap.' The irony was, that while he had been contriving his elaborate plot, the Doctor was straying into a trap of his own making.

Shawl draped over her head, shoulders hunched, spine bent almost double, impersonating the old crone, the Rani opened the bath house door.

'Get on in. Get on in,' she cackled. 'Towels are already there.'

Four miners trooped in and slouched into the bath chamber. Three of them began to undress. The fourth commenced a tour of inspection. Unfortunately, by the time he discovered the pipe, crimson steam was already billowing into the room. As his comrades collapsed, he tried to fan away the fumes, but the anaesthetic was too potent. Resistance grew feeble . . . and the Doctor sunk protestingly into oblivion . . .

8

Face to Face

Titanium hoops shackled the Doctor's wrists. A blanket covered his torso. Only his head was exposed as he lay on the trolley. Unconscious. Vulnerable.

Having connected the miner on the other trolley to the computer and the extractor so that the fluid from his brain would drip into the crystal flagon, the Rani crossed to the Doctor.

Thinking he was just another human, she brushed the tendrils of fair curly hair from behind his left ear, ready to attach the nozzle of the extracting tube.

Stopped.

Touched his skin. It felt too cool.

Perplexed, she picked up a spontaneous thermometer bracelet: a sensor of her own design. She placed it on the Doctor's forehead. Sixty, flashed on its read-out. She shook it, tested again. Sixty degrees, the temperature of a Time Lord, not that of a human.

Still not wholly convinced, she bent to listen on the left side of his chest where the human heart is found. Then she listened on the right side. There, too, was the steady beat of a heart. *Two* hearts! This had to be a Time Lord. And she knew who!

Brusquely she swabbed the coal dust from his face with a wet sponge. The icy dowsing brought the Doctor round.

The blue eyes widened with dawning recognition as he saw the figure crouching over him.

'Well, well, well. The Rani.'

'You were expecting to see the Master?' Annoyed

though she was with the Doctor's encroachment, she could not suppress a glacial glint of satisfaction at his futile attempts to release the clamped wrists.

'See? Not exactly. Not unless he's grown a little larger since I last saw him!' On that last encounter, the Master, hoist by his own petard, was being reduced to the size of a microbe!

'Your smugness is misplaced. He's here. He's normal size. And he wants you dead – curse the pair of you!'

Despite his struggles, the Doctor failed to loosen the straps. A change of tack. A critical appraisal of the Rani's costume.

'Can't say I approve of your taste in clothes. Doesn't do a thing for you, that outfit.'

'Your regeneration's not too attractive either!'

'Brain regeneration's what I need!' The Doctor meant what he said. He should have been able to pin this down to the Rani. Personality changes probably due to the imbalance of body chemicals ought to have led him to suspect the Rani. Her knowledge of chemistry was second to none. What's more, he knew she'd been banished from Gallifrey and was roaming the Universe. But what was she doing here? Pointless to ask. She'd never tell him. He was going to have to elicit the information by more subtle means.

'Well, you had me fooled if that's any consolation.'

'It isn't.'

His opinion was a matter of indifference to the Rani. All that disturbed her was his limitless capacity for meddling. She needed the brain fluid. He, with his sentimental affection for the earthlings, was bound to try and impede her.

'Of course you'd have been discovered eventually,' the Doctor persisted. 'Even without my intervention.'

'I never have.'

'Oh, this isn't your first visit then?'

'I've been coming to this wretched planet for cen-

58

turies.'

'Without being caught? I'm impressed. You must be a brilliant tactician as well as a brilliant chemist.'

'It isn't difficult. These homo sapiens you so admire are a feckless lot. Always in disarray. The Trojan Wars, Julius Caesar, the American War of Independence.'

'And now the Luddite Riots.'

'Perfect cover.'

For what? He looked about the laboratory, assessing then diagnosing the Rani's impedimenta: the monitor with a bisection of a skull representation, the pulsating tubes linked to the miner, and then the crystal flagon receiving miniscule droplets.

While he was marshalling his thoughts, the Rani was punching up the scanner. On the screen was a deserted meadow. This was not what she wanted to see. Impatiently she altered the co-ordinates.

'I think I've got it!' By collating the data he'd resolved the conundrum. 'You're extracting a chemical from the brain. The result is the victims become aggressive, violent. Can't rest – that's it! The chemical that promotes sleep!'

The deduction aggravated the Rani. 'I begin to understand why the Master finds you such a menace!' She jabbed at the scanner again. An empty approach road filled the screen. 'Where is the idiot?'

'I presume you're referring to the Master.' The Doctor's jovial tone belied his mounting sense of desperation. His voyage of discovery had brought to light a gruesome situation; one that he could do nothing to reverse. He was a prisoner.

'Well, since I don't want to be a nuisance to you, why not release me?'

It was a fatuous try and was treated with disdain. The Rani continued her search for the Master.

'Traditionally you've wished this planet no ill.' This is what puzzled the Doctor. The Rani, unlike the

Master, had never deliberately set out to be destructive. If anything or anyone got in the way of her experiments, she would remove it, or them. But there would have to be a reason.

'I don't now. It's simply that they've got the sole source of supply –'

'Source of supply!' The Doctor's anger exploded. 'These are human beings, Rani. Living creatures who've done you no harm!'

'What harm have the animals in the fields done them?' The Rani was stabbing the vermilion tabs on the scanner. 'The rabbits they snare? Sheep they nourish to slaughter? They're carnivores. Do they worry about the lesser species when they sink their teeth into a lamb chop?'

The barren logic of the scientist seemed faultless. Before the Doctor could deploy his facility for exhuming fallacy, he was thwarted. The Rani had located the Master in the vicinity of the pit. Quickly donning her shawl, she turned to the nearest assistant. 'Josh, guard him!'

The Doctor glanced at the muscular individual who moved in response. So, this was the missing Josh who had not been seen since he came off shift.

The Rani concluded her directive. 'If he tries to escape, kill him.' About to leave, she had a better idea. 'No, Josh, don't kill the Doctor.' She indicated the miner on the adjacent trolley. 'Kill *him*.' A smile. '*Touché*, Doctor?'

It was indeed a clever ruse. The Doctor would now do nothing while she was away for fear of jeopardising the miner's life.

'Don't hurry back,' he called to her retreating figure.

Peri saw the old crone hobble from the bath house. Exhortations to stay put had gone unheeded. She had followed the Doctor.

60

It had not been the happiest of experiences. She felt like a leper. The besieged villagers, normally friendly, were hostile. A sensitive girl, she did not blame them. Nobody could cope with the trauma of having husbands and sons mutated into marauding savages. Shattered windows were a stark reminder of the mindless terror assailing Killingworth.

When the old crone reached the bottom of the hill, Peri abandoned the shelter of an alley and crossed the street.

Tentatively, she entered the hallway. 'Doctor?'

No reply.

She advanced into the bath chamber. 'Doctor?' I know you're here. I'd've seen you leave otherwise –' Shocked, she saw the two drugged bodies sprawled on the reed mats . . . the parted wall at the far end . . . Nervously, she skirted the unconscious men and apprehensively ventured through the wall.

The scene that greeted her was even more distressing; the Doctor shackled to a trolley. 'Doctor –!' She started forward.

'Stop!' The bellow halted Peri in her tracks.

'What d'you mean, stop? I'm going to free you.'

'No!' The Rani's two assistants were standing quite impassively, but the Doctor had seen enough to realise they were conditioned to obey her orders. Implicitly. Without mercy. Josh may once have been the husband of the gentle young woman and father of her gurgling, six month old baby, but not any more. Now he was the Rani's puppet. 'Touch me and their orders are to kill!'

'But I can't just – I must do something!' She banged her hips in frustration.

'You can.' The Doctor waggled his head towards the miner. 'Get that poor fellow out of here.' He had calculated that Josh would obey his instructions to the letter.

'How?'

'Use some of that famous American initiative! Push him outside!'

Peri was confused. Wouldn't the Doctor be putting himself in peril if she touched the other trolley?

'Their orders relate only to me. Now move, Peri!'

Keeping a wary eye on the two muscular assistants, Peri eased past and began wheeling the trolley from the laboratory. She hesitated. 'Orders? Whose orders?'

'Just for once forget the cross examination and go!' There was no mistaking the urgency.

Peri guided the trolley into the bath chamber. Straining, puffing, she manoeuvred round the recumbent bodies –

The latch rattled on the street door. She froze.

In walked the old crone. Peri stuttered as she fought to offer the elderly lady an explanation.

The words were still-born. Standing beside the old crone was the person she most feared!

A beatific smile transformed the Master's pale visage as he registered Peri's presence.

'Who's this brat?' asked the Rani.

'My dear Rani, quite unwittingly you have made my triumph utterly complete.' He paused, luxuriating in the moment. 'Allow me to introduce Miss Perpugilliam Brown, the Doctor's latest travelling companion. Although her travelling days will soon be over . . .'

9

Triumph Of The Master

Bandana streaming, on the wings of fear, a tinker fled. Hurdling fence and brook, he swiftly outpaced Jack Ward and his gang of aggressors. The hunt was desultory; the prize they sought was the tinker's abandoned cart. Scattering copper kettles, pots and pans, they dumped the TARDIS on board and dragged it tumultuously along the rutted lanes to Killingworth.

Terrified villagers retreated into their cottages. The lame and the infirm, slow to get out of their path, were clubbed to the ground. A nine year old boy, recognising his father, ran to him and received an ear-ringing clout. Discordantly, the jeering mob chanted a mocking parody of a funeral march. The corpse to be buried was the TARDIS.

That was not the only bereavement the Master had in mind!

'I thought he was dead.' Peri had been prodded into the laboratory and her protest was addressed to the Doctor.

The Master answered, 'As you observe, I'm very much alive.' He glanced at the shackled prisoner. 'Your erstwhile mentor, on the other hand, is about to – I believe the modern expression is "snuff the candle"!'

'Snuff the candle! You know, you've always lacked style!' The ridicule was a bluff; the Doctor's attempt to defer what now seemed inevitable. A slender hope; especially with the Rani there. Summary execution was her style!

'Stop the babbling and get on with it!' she insisted.

'I've a score to settle first!' The Master turned to Peri.

She knew the score to which he was referring. It was a memory she had never been able to eradicate.

'When we last met, you could have saved me. Instead you left me to die!' He trained the TCE on the petrified girl.

'No!' Respite came from an unexpected quarter. 'Don't kill the girl.'

'Thank you, Rani.' Sincerity and relief. 'I'm glad you haven't sunk quite to the Master's depths,' said the Doctor.

His gratitude was misplaced. The Rani checked Peri's pulse.

'Hey, let go of me!'

'Human.'

'So?' The significance missed the Master.

'Her brain's as good as anyone else's.'

Willingly he lowered the TCE. This was an un-anticipated bonus; an opportunity to add to his rival's torment. 'No comment, Doctor?'

'I don't think I could stand it.' He was still playing the only gambit available, but Peri was puzzled by the jocular repartee.

'Stand what?'

'A hyperactive Peri. It's too ghastly to contemplate.'

Despite lacking knowledge of the Rani's activities, Peri had little doubt that she was in for a decidedly unpleasant experience. So how could the Doctor go on being frivolous?

It was no problem for the Master. 'We're being treated to an example of his famous sense of humour,' he explained. 'I'm afraid, Doctor, even that will desert you soon.'

Before eliminating his loathed adversary, he intended to turn the screw; orchestrate his suffering to a crescendo. Peri's future was determined; she would be given to the Rani. But what of the Doctor's favourite planet? 'A turbulent time, Doctor, in Earth's history?'

'Not one of its most serene, I agree.'

'A critical period?'

'You could say that.'

'Oh, I do. The beginning of a new era.' He sought Peri's opinion. 'Why do you think that should happen now?'

'I guess I've never given it much thought.' She was mesmerised by the Rani's clinical preparations with the brain extractor. She had no concept of what the tubes and the crystal flagon were for, but this cold-blooded woman gave her the shivers!

'Ah, but you should.' He caressed the left side of Peri's neck, knowing that soon the tube would be grafted there. 'I'm talking about the impact of the individual. Has not your country based its philosophy on the cult of the individual.

Repelled by his black-gloved touch, Peri recoiled.

The contemptuous exposition droned on: 'A sentimental concept that squanders the opportunities presented by the exceptional gifts of these men of genius.'

'Doctor, do you get his drift?'

'Only too well, Peri.' Indeed he did! The mosaic was complete and the picture formed had at its centre the forthcoming meeting: the congress of George Stephenson's talented contemporaries.

'He wants to pervert history!' Peri suddenly realised.

'I'm afraid the Prince of Darkness here would not see it as perversion.'

'Maudlin claptrap!' A vehement reply from the Master. Travelling Time Lords were forbidden to interfere with events on earth, but he rejected such edicts. Why should he observe the rules of Gallifrey? He'd been cast out and no longer recognised the Council's jurisdiction. 'The talents of these geniuses should be harnessed to a superior vision. With their help, I can turn this insignificant planet into a powerbase unique in the Universe!'

Mustering all the self control he could, the Doctor tried to maintain his pretence of nonchalance – an attitude that might incite the Master to overplay his hand. 'And you intend to use the Rani's bag of tricks to achieve this egocentric scheme.'

'You are indeed a worthy opponent, Doctor. It is what gives your destruction its piquancy!'

Nevertheless, the Doctor's condescending stoicism was beginning to rankle. The Master pressed the vermilion tabs of the scanner.

'Excellent! Feast your eyes, Doctor, on the imminent demise of the TARDIS!' He swivelled the scanner round.

'Demise?' Peri could see the TARDIS being shunted through the village.

'Death! Destruction! Finito TARDIS! How's that for style?' The Master's exuberance knew no bounds.

'Doctor, if they destroy the TARDIS –'

The Doctor cut in. 'Very clever. Optical illusion recreated on the screen. I've tried that but never succeeded.'

'It's no illusion!' The Master's affirmation was unequivocal.

'I hope you're right, Doctor.' Troubled, Peri watched the progress of the TARDIS along the street.

'He's not.' Uncompromising dismissal from the Rani.

'Believe me I am, Peri. The Rani's cleverer than any of us. She's obviously been able to modify this scanner so that it reflects what is in the mind instead of what is happening in reality –'

'Push!' The Master had had enough.

'The – the trolley?' Peri felt disorientated. What the heck was happening?

He levelled the TCE. 'One false move . . .'

'Push it where?'

'Outside.'

'No!' The Rani was too astute to be gulled by the Doctor's ploy. 'He doesn't leave here.'

From his breast pocket, the Master yanked the phial of brain fluid and flaunted it before her. 'I wonder how many weeks of work this represents.'

Balefully, the Rani refused to concede.

'And how many of the Doctor's precious humans have contributed,' the Master continued.

Even in her confusion, Peri sensed everything hinged on the resolution of the confrontation.

The Rani accepted defeat. 'Do as he says.'

A magnanimous smile. 'You shall have the girl when we return.' The Master tucked the phial into his breast pocket, then brandished the TCE. 'Now, push! Unless you prefer a swifter end!'

Fear giving her added strength, Peri trundled the trolley through the bath chamber and into the hallway.

They reached the street just as the procession with its noisy pall bearers was passing. From their yells and roars, only the words 'pit' and 'shaft' could be distinguished.

'The Last Rites, Doctor!'

'I can't really see from this far away.'

'You can hear!'

Peri had given up. There was nothing anybody could do. Not even the Doctor, she thought.

She should have known better.

'I gather they're going to throw my TARDIS down the pit shaft.'

'All the way down to the bottom!' The words were mouthed with relish.

The shouts of the hyped-up aggressors grew louder as they neared the pit gates.

'Stop or we'll fire!'

The threat proved inflammatory. Using the cart as a battering ram, they recklessly smashed through the gates, scattering the guards in disarray.

'Nothing can stop them!' In his excitement, the Master failed to register that he not the fated Time Machine held the Doctor's attention.

Shots ricocheted. Casualties fell. But the defenders, forced to disperse, were unable to impede the cart's relentless progress towards the pit shaft.

Green darted ahead to remove the cover; a bulky wooden platform that fitted over the gaping hole to prevent accidents when a shift was finished. Baying with triumph, the brawny aggressors hoisted the TARDIS from the cart and heaved it over the edge . . .

The Master's elation overwhelmed him. Momentarily. That moment was all the Doctor needed.

A sharp kick – and the TCE flew from the Master's grasp.

'Shove, Peri! Shove!'

Galvanised into action, Peri shoved – but in her eagerness, instead of pushing the trolley uphill away from the pit, she pushed it downhill.

'Wrong way!' The Doctor's cry came too late. Gathering momentum, the cumbersome vehicle sped down the slope.

She sprinted after it, but her pace could not match the runaway.

The trolley bumped on, shaving trees, threatening to collide with boulders and posts that would capsize it with bone-fracturing impact. Able only to raise his head, the Doctor was scared. Above, foliage became a blurred mass punctuated by dazzling rays of sunlight.

Then luck smiled on him. A group of miners stepped onto the path. To his relief, they caught the trolley and brought it to a halt.

'Thank you, gentlemen. I'm most grateful. Now if you'd release me –' He faltered. The neck of the nearest miner had the tell-tale crimson mark.

Peri, still chasing, was approaching.

'Stay back, Peri! Stay back!' The Doctor had identified another of the saviours – Jack Ward.

'Now it's your turn! You can join your diabolical box!' They swung him in the direction of the shaft and began running . . . faster . . . and faster . . .

'Let him go! Let him go!' Peri's pleas had no effect as she tore after them. Their death lust was not to be denied.

From his hilltop position, the Master felt sure the humiliations of the past were about to be avenged.

The trelliswork of timbers and the giant wheel above the shaft loomed ominously into the Doctor's restricted view. A final mighty thrust – and the hapless Time Lord accelerated inexorably towards the yawning black hole . . .

10

A Change Of Loyalty

Sleeves rolled up, a man was concertinaing creaking bellows to rekindle the forge fire. As he paused and dragged a rag from his thick leather belt to wipe the sweat from his brow, he heard Peri's screams.

In reflex, he turned, took in the situation and sprang for the pit.

The trolley's momentum would have made arresting it a physical impossibility. Astutely realising this, the man ran for the shaft.

It was even money who would reach the gaping hole first. The stake? The Doctor's life.

Lungs pumping, the man kicked the bulky cover into position. Relentlessly the trolley came on. He fumbled with the stay. It clicked home as the wheels jarred into the cover, braking . . .

When the reverberations subsided, the Doctor's vision came into focus. Despite the agape mouth sucking in air, there was about his rescuer a piercing intelligence emanating from rugged, plebeian features.

The Doctor's thanks were profuse. But for this stranger's quick thinking, he would now be spinning to his death in the bowels of the earth.

'Are't tha' hurt? Harmed at all?' The solicitude was genuine.

'No. A trifle cramped.'

'Aye . . . Aye. Tha' would be.'

'It's these straps.'

Instead of releasing the clamps, the stranger was feeling their texture. 'Aye, I suppose . . . Intriguing.'

'The straps? Yes, well that's a long story.'

'This metal. I've nay seen the like of it afore. Dost know which foundry forged it?'

In the midst of a calamity, what sort of individual would be so diverted as to enquire about the composition of a metal? Recognising only too well the impulse, the Doctor beamed.

'George Stephenson, I presume.'

'Aye, I'm Stephenson.'

'An enormous pleasure to meet you, sir.' The Doctor lifted a shackled wrist as far as he could and Stephenson gripped the fingers in a warm handshake. 'Would you be kind enough to undo these straps?'

Stephenson complied. 'Forgive me. T'were metal that took my attention.' This was understandable. The titanium the Rani had used was not known in the nineteenth century. If it had been, many inventors would have benefited. Especially George Stephenson who was experimenting with steam engines and would eventually design the famous Rocket.

'Run, Doctor! Run!' Peri's warning preceded her panting arrival.

The Doctor looked back as he slid from the trolley. Jack Ward and the aggressors were returning to the attack. Intent on slaughter, they would spare none of them. 'Quickly, we've got to get away!'

'Follow me.' Stephenson hared off.

Drawn by the racket of the fracas, Ravensworth was at the breached pit entrance surveying the shambles of the battle.

Ripped from its hinges, the gate was beyond repair. Already villagers were drifting in. Ravensworth knew he could not count on their loyalty. Understandably. The attackers, however demented, were their kinfolk. His pressing task was to secure the mine area.

'On the gate!' he commanded a guard. 'No-one

enters or leaves! That's an order!'

A second guard was rubbing his bruises.

'Here! Take this!' Ravensworth gave him his blunderbuss. 'Round up all the able-bodied men you can. Search the pit. I want every one of those scoundrels hunted down!'

A crowd of bystanders surrounded a sentry whose wounds were being dressed by Luke.

'How bad is it?'

'Can't tell, m'lord. Lost a great deal of blood.'

'Where's Stephenson?'

'In't forge. I were on't way over when I heard noise.'

'Find him. Tell him to stay in the workshop until those ruffians are under restraint.'

'Shall I finish binding –'

'*Now!*' On the double, Luke obeyed.

'You!' Ravensworth summoned the drayman. 'Make yourself useful. Staunch the bleeding while I get a bandage from the office.'

He stalked away. The guards watched his departure. So did the Master. His simmering fury fuelled his determination to extirpate his rival. He must get into the pit before its defences were reassembled.

Handicapped by her costume, Peri had difficulty in keeping up as Stephenson and the Doctor fled through a haphazard muddle of buildings, wagons, stables and loading bays.

'Come on, Peri! Come on! We haven't lost them yet!'

A predatory holler confirmed the Doctor's declaration. Their pursuers still had the scent.

In a grain store, they disturbed a furry swarm of feasting vermin. Peri gulped, closed her eyes and ploughed on; she tried not to think of the long skirt brushing the floorboards.

They had almost reached the workshop when Luke blundered into them.

'Mr Stephenson, his lordship says –'

'Lift planks!'

Luke shifted a couple of planks at the rear of the workshop.

'Inside!'

Unceremoniously, Stephenson bundled Peri and the Doctor through the hole.

Scrambling in after them, Stephenson and Luke slotted the planks into their fixings.

The workshop's major exhibit was a prototype railway engine. Rough wooden benches claimed the rest of the limited space. Jotted calculations and primitive tools cluttered their surfaces.

'His lordship told me to keep –'

Stephenson motioned Luke to silence. With bated breath, they listened to their pursuers thumping past. Only then did they relax.

'Somewhat unorthodox entry,' remarked the Doctor.

'Lord Ravensworth's notion,' said Stephenson. 'He thought we should be prepared lest the Luddite riots started here. Seems he were right.'

'Except these men are not Luddites,' came the Doctor's reply.

'They're not?'

'No. That's what you're meant to believe.'

'Then why did they attack thee?'

'Assumed I was attending this meeting of yours.'

'And for that they were prepared to kill thee?'

'Afraid so. Not just me either.'

Luke knew this assertion to be true. 'That's what I were trying to tell thee,' he added. 'Tha's to stay in't workshop, his lordship says. He's feared for safety of thee and rest of visitors.'

'Tha' means Davy, Faraday, Telford and t'others are in danger?'

'Don't you?' asked the Doctor.

'Nay, I find that incredible!'

74

'If tha'd seen devastation at gate tha' wouldn't, sir.'

'You can't reject the evidence, Stephenson.'

Peri joined in. 'That's not the first time they've tried to kill the Doctor either!'

''Tis truth.' Luke's golden hair shone in the light from the wicker lamp that burned in the anarchic workshop. His earnest young face wore a worried frown.

Stephenson began to waver. 'Dost reckon us should cancel meeting?'

The Doctor was in no doubt.

'Luke?'

'Aye, sir. I do.'

Peri certainly thought so.

Stephenson capitulated. 'A pity.' He crossed to a bench. 'I suspect Doctor's contribution would've put cat among pigeons. Where's paper, lad?'

Luke ripped a sheet from a pad. Picking up a quill, Stephenson began to write.

'Fine. Now that's sorted out,' Peri said to the Doctor. 'Shouldn't we do something about the TARDIS?'

Paying no heed, the Doctor gazed around the workshop with its crude implements, and was consumed with respect for the inventor. Without the more refined equipment of Peri's twentieth century, George Stephenson's ingenuity would reshape existence on the planet Earth – provided, that is, the Master and the Rani could be foiled. It was a grim thought but not one that prevented him from being intrigued by the prototype engine.

'The Blucher, is it?' he asked Luke.

'Aye.'

'Doctor, this is no time to be playing trains!'

'Mind if I take a peep?'

'The TARDIS is at the bottom of that pit shaft!' Peri wasn't going to be fobbed off.

'We have to wait –' his voice became muffled as he

stuck his head into the boiler of the engine, '– until it's safe.'

'And that could be forever!'

Speaking quietly, Luke moved closer to Peri. 'When Doctor were attacked again . . .' he faltered, reluctant to hear the answer to his question.

'Yes, Luke?'

'Was – did me Da' take part?'

Peri nodded.

'I asked me Mam about that red mark. On his neck. She knew nowt of it. She'd nay seen it. Dost know what caused it?'

Selfconsciously, Peri rubbed her own neck, recalling that she, too, was almost a victim.

Stephenson interrupted. 'Luke, take this to his lordship.' He gave him the note he had written.

'Dost mind if I also seek me Da'?'

'Of course not, lad.'

'Wait!' The Doctor crawled from under the Blucher. 'Luke, your father's not the man you knew. Take care . . .'

Perplexed, the young apprentice left. Stephenson was also perturbed by the Doctor's warning. 'I'd nay like anything to happen to Luke. Lad's got great future. He'll outshine me.'

This final remark worried the Doctor. It bewildered Peri. 'You?' How could Luke Ward outshine George Stephenson? No-one had done that – not according to the history books.

Stephenson continued. 'I were down pit at nine. Never did get much schooling. But Lord Ravensworth's seen to it Luke's been well taught. We've both great hopes for the lad.'

Little did he know how tragically forlorn these hopes were to be.

Having gained access, the Master was systematically

76

searching the sprawling environs of the mine when he witnessed a dispute that suggested an entirely new strategy.

'Hey, Tim! Tim Bass! Hast seen me Da'?' Luke had spotted the marauding aggressor flitting between the sheds, obviously avoiding the guards.

The jaunty scarf was still tied about Tim's brow but his jovial manner had been banished. 'He'll want nowt to do with thee! Not as long as tha's lackey to that Stephenson!'

'But why? He's nay objected afore.'

'He do now. Assistant! Traitor more like! Out of road!' He jostled the slim apprentice aside and blustered on.

Bewildered, Luke stared after him. What had happened to the happy-go-lucky Tim Bass, a man rarely without a smile? There was a red mark below his ear. Could that have something to do with his ugly mood?

'Excuse me, young man.' Luke was accosted by a gentleman expensively attired in a black velvet suit trimmed with silver. 'I've been invited here by Lord Ravensworth.' The gentleman dangled a medallion between his fingers. 'Can you tell me where I'll find him?' The medallion was swinging . . . rhythmically . . . gleaming hypnotically . . .

The scene was being observed but, alas for Luke, not by someone who would help him. The Rani was at her scanner.

With bleak disapproval, she saw the Master take out the box of maggots he had filched from her. She had seen enough! Fretfully, she ripped out the plug, blanking the screen. The imbecile had ruined everything!

Venting her spleen on Josh, she ordered him to dismantle the laboratory.

Selecting a fluorescent maggot, the Master tickled

Luke's lips with the slimy parasite. It squirmed repulsively yet Luke did not flinch.

'Luke, I want you to swallow this very special sweetmeat.'

Without even a shudder, the hypnotised youth sucked in the wriggling grub, chewed, then swallowed.

A blue glow suffused his pupils.

'Splendid. You have a note I see.'

'Aye. 'Tis for his lordship.'

'Give it to me.'

After reading Stephenson's advice to cancel the meeting, the Master knew the task his newly created acolyte could perform.

'Luke, this meeting is *not* to be cancelled. Do you understand?'

'I understand.' A slight reserve was the only manifestation of the change in Luke, and that would be interpreted as shyness even by those who were familiar with him.

'If anyone tries to prevent it, you destroy them! Is that clear?'

'That is clear.' His subservience was absolute.

'Anyone, Luke. Anyone at all!'

11

Fools Rush In

'The key is more power.'

George Stephenson and the Doctor were crawling under the Blucher. 'If I can increase that, speeds of fifteen, maybe twenty miles an hour become possible. Aye, power's t'problem.'

The Doctor longed to be able to enlighten the inventor, but he dared not. That would be influencing history. Could he, he wondered, just give a hint?

'Doctor, there *is* a more pressing problem!' chided Peri.

Reluctantly he squeezed out from beneath the engine, scrubbing a patch of oil from his turquoise cravat. 'You're correct, of course. Let's go.'

As he lifted the loosened planks for her to leave the workshop, Peri thought, for once, they were in accord. She was mistaken. Her reference related to the TARDIS stuck at the bottom of that shaft and without which they were stranded. His worry was the crucial matter of Earth's destiny.

Someone else was brooding, but on a less grand scale. Jack Ward blamed the Doctor for his present plight. Using his knowledge of the hotchpotch of sheds, he had managed to evade capture.

'It's nay right having to skulk round like criminals,' he grouched to his mate, Dobbs. 'Guards everywhere!' They were in the bagging compound where they had sought temporary shelter. 'Just because of that poxy rogue in't yellow trousers!' He whacked the scales in

79

frustration. 'Well, he's in't pit somewhere.' All Jack wanted was a chance to square the account.

The chance came. With characteristic imprudence, the Doctor strutted across a quadrangle parallel to the compound. Signalling to Dobbs, Ward began to stalk his unwary adversary.

Hampered by the voluminous skirt, Peri lagged behind in what was, for her, an unappetising sight-seeing tour.

'Hey, less haste, more speed!' Her faith in his sense of direction, literally and metaphorically, was less than a hundred per cent.

She had a point. Anticipating the Doctor's more circuitous route, Ward, familiar with every nook and cranny, took a short-cut to the overhead track etched against the skyline. Nimble as a cat, he scaled the framework, then lay in wait.

Still trailing in the rear, Peri was disgruntled. Why the heck had she ever gotten herself into this fix? Adventures were all very well so long as they had a happy ending. Happy ending! In despair, she cast her gaze up to the heavens – and glimpsed a figure easing a tipping bolt from the socket of a stationary loaded truck. Plumb below, having paused to get his bearings, stood the Doctor!

'Doc –!' A beefy palm clapped over her mouth killing the warning as Ward braced himself to tip the truck.

Eyes boggling over Dobbs's stifling hand, she was a distraught spectator as Ward sent several tons of coal cascading onto his unsuspecting victim.

A more colourful turbulence was depicted on the room-divider screen that remained in the Rani's now denuded laboratory. Painted in the style of Turner's 'Eruption of Souffrier', it portrayed, in sultry ambers and vivid scarlets, a smouldering volcano. A chilling antithesis, the Rani was arranging the exotic mural with meticulous delicacy. It dominated the bare room; every item of scientific apparatus had been removed.

The click of the latch. 'At last you're back, you incompetent egoist! Give me my phial!' The sour greeting was for the Master.

'And I thought you were waiting for me.' A lie. The Master had no illusions about the Rani.

'If I didn't need that brain fluid desperately, I'd've put light years between us!'

'What better reason could I have for keeping it?'

'You'll play that card once too often! With you on the scene I might be wiser to cut my losses and go!'

Quelling a tinge of alarm over the possibility, the Master changed from banter to bribery. 'Read this.' He gave her the note taken from Luke.

A perfunctory glance. 'So the meeting's been cancelled.' She was unimpressed. All she'd agreed to do was help get rid of the Doctor.

'No. This was never delivered.' He snatched the note. 'You disappoint me. A scientist, yet you're not thinking objectively.' He recited the names of the inventors. 'Over twenty men of genius! Have you no conception of what we could do if we controlled them?'

Her indifference should have stemmed the flow. It did not. The bombast continued unabated. 'Harness their genius and this planet could become the platform for the most devastating power in the Universe!'

'You're forgetting, I already rule a planet. Miasimia Goria.'

'I'm forgetting nothing!' This Machiavelli had anticipated her response. 'Help me and I promise you all the facilities you need!'

An astute offer. The Rani listened.

'Instead of sneaking back here in disguise, you will be able to set up a laboratory and process as many humans as you choose! A hundred. A thousand. There are millions of them!'

81

His cynicism began to erode her hostility. This new proposal had its advantages. Having to establish processing laboratories every visit was abysmally tedious. But she was not to be won over that readily. 'What guarantee would I have?'

'My need. That unique box of parasites will not go far. Only you have the formula.'

The Rani was almost persuaded . . . but there was a flaw. 'The Time Lords will never permit it!'

'And who is going to alert them?'

Who indeed? Not the Doctor. She'd make sure of that! Unlike her incompetent partner, she was going to allow their adversary to take the initiative. These earthlings had a saying: 'fools rush in where angels fear to tread'. She considered the Doctor to be a fearless fool.

When the dust had settled, all that could be seen where the 'fearless fool' had stood was a smothering pile of coal.

Peri, still captive, scratched and kicked in an effort to get free and salvage the Doctor before he was suffocated. Tame submission was not her style, but sadly her strength did not match her spirit. Dobbs restrained her with ease.

'Let lass go or I'll blow brains out!' The barrel of a flintlock pistol was rammed into Dobbs's temple by a patrolling guard. 'You, too, Jack Ward. Come down from there!'

Released, Peri began clawing frantically at the mountain of coal –

'You're making a frightful mess of that pretty dress.'

The Doctor's voice! Clear, unmuffled, not from the grave! She turned – to be rewarded with a genial smile as he stepped out from behind a stanchion.

'I thought . . . the coal . . . how did you? . . . I mean, you were directly underneath!'

'Peripheral vision. All I needed was a split second's grace.' He sounded more casual than he felt. He had learned the technique from the Shikari, on the Planet of the Hunters. It enabled him to see not just what was in front, but in a much wider arc. He contemplated the pyramid of coal. Without the art of peripheral vision, that would have been his burial mound.

A more blinkered vision was being employed in the laboratory where the Rani was ensuring that all evidence of her occupancy, except the room-divider, had been whisked away. A final adjustment to the spectacular mural and she was satisfied.

'Haven't you forgotten something?' The Master indicated the two assistants passively awaiting her bidding. 'You can hardly take them out onto the streets.'

'No. You're right. I can't.'

The Rani might almost have been swotting flies for all the emotion she displayed as she tapped the annihilating code on her mini-computer.

Josh and his companion clutched at their throats. Excruciating pain forced them to cry out. But the crimson mark continued to spread until it had throttled them to death . . .

12

An Unpleasant Surprise

Chafing the crimson scar that blemished his neck, Ward preceded Dobbs into Ravensworth's office.

'Only two! What about the others?'

The guard, holding his gun on the two aggressors, was chastened by his employer's reprimand; he had been expecting praise. 'Don't know, m'lord.'

'Got away, you mean!'

'Good luck to 'em!' The gun had not completely subdued Jack Ward.

'Be quiet, Ward.' The mine owner's ire was still reserved for the guard. 'My orders were to round up the lot!'

'Us hasn't finished yet!' came Ward's interjection.

'I said that's enough!' The peer was florid with anger. He had never experienced such insubordination. Crass insolence from an employee struck at the very roots of nineteenth-century society.

But the mutated miner was not now a product of that age. He grabbed a chair to hurl at Ravensworth.

'Do that Jack Ward and I'll blow tha's arm off!' The gun was cocked.

Baffled, resentful, Ward let the chair drop.

'Tie him up!' Lord Ravensworth was also confused. He deplored having to resort to these measures. They refuted the very philosophy that he had subscribed to since inheriting the colliery. Reason was the guiding beacon of this enlightened era, but now it seemed to be regressing to barbarism. His own doubts nagged. Should he have taken further action earlier? Sent for the militia? With the woods infested by these disturbed wretches, that option was no longer available. Killingworth was virtually cut off from the outside world.

A scuffle roused him from his introspection. Belligerently, Ward was straining at his bonds. To think this was the father of Luke; that gentle, reliable youth whose aspirations he'd so encouraged.

Totally subjugated to the Master's will, Luke impassively entered the workshop. Stephenson looked up from the iron flange he was heating in the furnace.

'Tha's delivered note?'

'Aye.' The deceit came without hesitation.

'What did his lordship say?'

'Nowt.' The second lie.

Stephenson, interpreting Luke's dull tone as being the result of a wigging from the boss, suffered a twinge of conscience. ''Appen I should've gone meself. Explained.' He rested the flange on the anvil. 'In't office, is he?'

'Nay!' The first stir of emotion from Luke. He dare not let the two men get together; his subterfuge would be discovered. 'Tha'll stay put. I'll fetch him to thee. 'Tis safer that way.'

The proposal placated Stephenson who had no cause to believe Luke was other than the considerate apprentice he had always been. 'Thanks, Luke. Tha's a real thoughtful lad . . .'

In the yard, there were further complications.

'Ah, Luke. I want a word with Stephenson. About this meeting.' Lord Ravensworth was en route for the workshop.

Luke had to stop him. 'He's nay in't workshop.'

'No?' Ravensworth was surprised. 'Where is he?'

'Down pit.' Mendacity was no longer foreign to Luke's nature. 'Wanted to arrange for visitors to see

86

demonstration.' A plausible explanation. 'What about meeting, m'lord?'

'In my opinion it should be called off.'

Luke's face betrayed none of the emotion this assertion triggered. Surging through his head came the Master's mandate: 'If anyone tries to prevent the meeting, you destroy them!' Surreptitiously, his fingers closed over a crowbar lodged on a crate.

'All this rampant brutality. We've no right to subject these people to such danger.' Lord Ravensworth was oblivious of his own proximity to danger.

'Mr Stephenson don't see any danger.' Despite the urge to kill, Luke continued to opt for persuasion. Perhaps there remained a spark of the original young man who rejected violence. 'Going to be fair disappointed he is if meeting doesn't take place. Eager to show off latest engine.' The crowbar was firmly grasped ready to strike.

'Somewhat selfish reasoning.' The censorious Ravensworth had no inkling of the dark forces haunting his protégé.

'Not if he's convinced they'll come to nay harm, your lordship.'

As he awaited a decision, Luke's muscles tensed . . . his patron's life hung in the balance . . .

'Convinced, you say? Ah well, George Stephenson has always enjoyed my complete trust.' A reluctant shrug. 'On his head be it.'

The fingers relaxed.

Ravensworth turned to leave, then changed his mind. 'However . . .'

The grip on the crowbar tightened again.

'Be sure to tell him what I've said.'

'Aye. I will.'

This time his lordship did depart.

If Ravensworth, albeit unwittingly, was distancing

himself from danger, the Doctor was doing the opposite. At least, that was Peri's vociferous conclusion.

'You can't be serious! You've only just escaped from there!'

The Doctor was advancing on the bath house. 'The victim returns to the scene of the crime.'

His gallows humour failed to amuse Peri. 'Look, let's be sensible about this.' She was terrified. 'Concentrate on getting the TARDIS out of that pit shaft.' Unbelievably, the Doctor unlocked the door and nipped in! Trailing after him, Peri's voice lowered to a whisper. 'Instead of shoving our necks into the noose again!'

Her forebodings carried no weight. The Doctor made straight for the bath chamber. He did at least stuff a towel into the gas pipe before examining the wall that partitioned off the laboratory.

'What if the Master and that awful Rani are inside?'

'They won't be.' Was the Doctor as confident as he sounded? He certainly seemed sure of himself as he went into the hallway again.

With his usual lack of explanation, he began investigating his surroundings. ' "Cowards die many times before their deaths",' he quoted as he traced an indentation in the woodwork. ' "The valiant never taste of death but once". William Shakespeare.'

'What about that other piece you're so fond of spouting? "Discretion is the better part of valour." That's Shakespeare too!'

Absently, the Doctor conceded she had a point. 'Interesting fellow, the Bard. Must see him again – aaaah!' He pressed a concealed button. The wall slid apart.

Expecting trouble to emerge, Peri shied away.

'Control panel. Very unsophisticated. Not worthy of the Rani.' Despite his bravado, the Doctor was circumspect as he entered the laboratory.

The sight that greeted him dispelled all thoughts of his own safety. The two assistants were spread-eagled on the floor.

'Josh!' exclaimed the Doctor as he hurried to the pathetic corpse and felt its pulse.

'Is he . . .?'

He shook a grim negative. Sadly Peri stared at Josh's body and remembered his young wife and their baby. The Master had a lot to answer for!

The Doctor's verdict was different. 'Some of the Rani's handiwork, I imagine. Don't come any farther, Peri.' Tentatively, she had stepped over the threshold. 'The Rani's quite capable of leaving behind some very unpleasant surprises.'

Crouching, he settled onto his heels. The wanton assassination had staunched his reckless streak. Soberly, he commenced a rigorous visual scan of the laboratory.

'Why the devil have you brought us to this miserable dump?'

The Master's querulous complaint echoed in the darkness. Bent almost double, the Rani was penetrating the low tunnels of the disused mine.

'I didn't bring you. You chose to come!'

'Why here?'

'It was my original base before I set up operations in the bath house.'

Cobwebs brushed her shawl and coal dust scrunched beneath her shoes. In the interest of self preservation, the Master lingered near the entrance.

'Did we have to walk? Couldn't we have used your TARDIS?'

She paused at an intersection. 'My TARDIS is performing a more important function.'

The Rani's arrogance in keeping her own counsel rankled. He glared after her. 'Is it too much to ask what that function might be?'

Resuming her progress, she was monosyllabic: 'Yes.'

Still crouched on his heels, the Doctor was pondering the same question the Master had posed. That the Rani would be nearby, he was certain; the Master's possession of the brain fluid would guarantee that. The price for its restitution? The Doctor's death? How?

'The red mark,' Peri indicated the crimson band that had garrotted Josh. 'The Rani?'

He nodded.

'What was she going to do to me?'

'Drain the substance from your brain that enables you to sleep.'

'But the results! Those other men! Hasn't she any conscience?'

'Like so many scientists, she believes we're simply walking heaps of chemicals. There's no place for the soul in her scheme of things.' He rose and began to patrol the laboratory.

'Why? I mean – what would she want it for?'

'That's an aspect I haven't fathomed.'

'I knew the substance existed. Drug companies in the States and Switzerland are trying to reproduce it. Sleeping pills and tranquillisers would become obsolete if they could. People wouldn't need them any more.'

The Doctor was positive that alleviating human suffering couldn't be the Rani's objective!

'How come you know her?' asked Peri.

'The same way I know the Master.'

'But he's an exiled Time Lord.'

'Quite. Two of a kind.' Carefully avoiding contact with the ornate room-divider, he studied the turbulent volcanic landscape. 'Odd . . . Very odd . . .'

'What is?'

'This screen. I'd've said Turner's too passionate for the Rani's sterile taste.'

90

A forage in the cornucopian pocket of his coat yielded a ball of twine with a hook on the end.

'I guess she thought so too, since she's not taken it with her.'

Peri moistened her lips as, gingerly, with the dexterity of a bomb disposal expert, the Doctor fastened the hook onto the screen. Then, playing out the line, he withdrew to a far corner.

'Shall we?'

'Shall we what?'

'See if I've misjudged the Rani.' He jerked the line.

Instantly, the picture came alive.

The volcano erupted.

Yellow fumes spewed into the laboratory and billowed towards the Doctor . . .

13

Taken For A Ride

'Dichlorodiethyl sulphide!'

Sniffing, the Doctor retreated.

'Dio – what?'

'Mustard gas! Don't breathe it in, Peri! Whatever you do, don't breathe it in!'

The advice was unnecessary. She had heard of the lethal gas: a killer that had paved the battlefields with corpses in the First Great War of the twentieth century.

The noxious yellow cloud was swooping rapidly towards the Doctor's side of the laboratory. He charged for an uncontaminated gap.

Simultaneously, the volcano erupted again, belching out more acrid fumes and blocking the escape route.

From the comparatively unaffected entrance, Peri watched impotently as he retreated.

His back thudded into the wall. He was cornered. The gas hemmed him in. Smothering his nose and mouth in a capacious handkerchief, he bawled to Peri.

'M . . . s . . . s!'

'I didn't get that!' The fumes were beginning to spread to her side now.

The Doctor removed the handkerchief briefly. 'Masks!'

'Masks?' The word was clear but the intention was not.

'The Rani's assistants!' Wisps of the gas seeped into his nostrils. The effect was immediate. He retched and spluttered.

But the message had got through. The masks the assistants had worn were hitched to their waist belts.

However, their bodies were already being licked by the deadly vapour.

Turning away, Peri inhaled deeply then dashed for the nearest body. Holding her breath, eyes smarting and streaming, Peri fumbled to unclip the mask.

The volcano belched again.

The Doctor's cheeks bulged with the effort of keeping his nose and mouth plugged. Everything depended on Peri.

Adrenalin pumped into her veins inducing a clarity in the perception of events and time that enabled Peri to steady her trembling fingers. In a whirlwind of continuous action, she unhitched the mask, slipped it on, filled her lungs with the purified air, rushed to Josh, yanked the mask from his belt and hurled it across the laboratory to the Doctor.

He caught it and pulled it on.

'Thank you, Peri.' His gasped gratitude, filtered by the snout, was a muted bass. 'Street door.'

'Street door?' Her vowels were also a couple of registers lower.

'Open it! Ventilation! Quickly!'

She scampered into the hallway and flung the front door wide. The yellow fumes began dispersing.

Returning, she found the Doctor no longer hunched in the corner. Instead, he was prowling the screen. At least, he was prowling a wardrobe which the shifted screen had revealed.

An unprepossessing piece of slate grey bedroom furniture in a laboratory? Peri was puzzled.

The Doctor did not seem to be. The symbolic rings carved on its panels had a significance for him. His next move startled Peri. He tugged at the green fob-chain looped across his plaid waistcoat.

'Hey, that's the key to the TARDIS!'

Confidently, he inserted the key in the lock and the wardrobe door swung open.

A TARDIS.

Peri made the connection. The Rani's TARDIS! But, oh no! The Doctor was about to step inside!

'Suppose she's in there –!' He had disappeared! Afraid of being left behind, she forgot her fears and nipped in after him.

Similar in design to the Doctor's TARDIS, the predominate colour of the Rani's time-machine was silver. Glass shelves and cabinets crammed with flasks, syringes, pipettes and bottles of all descriptions lined the silver walls.

In the centre was the control console crowned with a thin, tubular, steel maze of concentric rings floating in space. But what aroused the Doctor's curiosity as he ripped off his mask were the five large specimen jars supported by five pillars arranged in a circle about the central dais. The jars contained embryos, curled foetuses preserved in glutinous liquid and in a state of suspended animation.

'Ah, embryos of the Tyrannosaurus Rex.'

Peri grimaced at the revolting semi-formed dinosaurs, their sharp teeth already protruding from elongated jaws. She knew the Tyrannosaurus Rex was extinct. So how could the Rani have got these five embryos?

'She's been back to the Cretaceous Age to collect them.' The Doctor tapped a container. The baby monster did not move. 'Nasty creatures. Vicious teeth. Bite your leg off and chew it up. Bones and all.'

Peri could well believe that!

'Ah!' His mercurial attention butterflied to the neat rows of chemicals and toxic substances. 'The Rani's a magpie. D'you realise, through these, we could tell just where in the cosmos she's visited?' He was reading the labels on the containers.

'How about where she is right now? Will they tell us

that?' Hugging the masks – the Doctor had dumped his on her – Peri nervously eyed the alien interior.

An array of dials, calibrated scales and interwoven glass piping that serviced a perforated turntable dotted with test-tubes, took the Doctor's roving attention. 'Novel approach to chromatography, utilising pi-mesons –'

Without warning, the maze of tubular rings began to rotate . . . to whirl round each other, corkscrewing, winding up and down.

'Peri, run!'

'Why? Where?'

'*Run!*' She ran!

In the laboratory she halted, waiting for the Doctor to emerge.

He didn't.

What did occur was devastating. Vertical strips of light on the Rani's TARDIS pulsated once . . . twice . . . thrice . . . then dematerialisation.

The wardrobe had gone.

And so had the Doctor.

Peri's heart sank. 'Now what's he done?'

The Doctor had not done anything.

The TARDIS had simply started up and de-materialised of its own accord.

'Incredible! Absolutely incredible! A TARDIS that operates on remote command. The Rani *is* a genius.' The praise was genuine. To think she could summon her TARDIS from wherever she happened to be! It was an achievement which had eluded him.

He scrutinised the pulsator. That was where he'd come to grief on the last occasion. Walloped into that tower. Where was it? Pisa?

The wardrobe materialised in the old mine as the Rani pressed the final tab of her mini-transmitter.

'You've discovered the means of operating a

TARDIS by remote control! Brilliant! Quite brilliant! In tandem, you and I will rule the Universe!'

The Rani gave the Master a withering look. This egoist would never rule the Universe. If anybody were to attain that, it would be her. And she'd need no help from him. Help? The man was nothing but a hindrance! Now she would have to take him into her TARDIS. Something she was reluctant to do.

The scratch of the key alerted the Doctor. He darted into a corridor.

Entering, the Rani discarded the old crone's drab apparel. Underneath, she was wearing her own clothes: skin-tight black leather trews, tapering into knee-high boots, were topped with a black leather, long sleeved jerkin decorated with a discreet motif in silver. The outfit clung to her trim form. This was the Rani as she chose to present herself.

Even the Master spared her an admiring glance; it was only a fleeting digression however. 'Do I detect a lack of enthusiasm?' he asked.

'Grandiose schemes of ruling the Universe will mean nothing if that dilettante Doctor is still at large!' said the Rani.

Dilettante? Him? The Doctor, eavesdropping from his concealed position, was affronted!

'Dratted man!' Having energised a scanner, the Rani was studying the laboratory on the monitor. She had expected to see the Doctor's asphyxiated corpse. Instead, all she could see were those of the assistants. She flicked off the scanner.

'Don't tell me you've botched something!' the Master taunted. 'What did you do? Leave a trap for the Doctor?'

Ignoring the jibe, she went to a cupboard and began sorting through a stack of discs.

'Is that why we couldn't use your TARDIS? Its

power was needed to operate the –'

'Here! Carry these!' She shoved several of the discs at him. 'And be careful!'

Her rudeness provoked only apprehension. 'Why? What are they?'

Just the question the Doctor himself wanted to ask. From his angle, they resembled frisbees and looked as harmless.

But they could not be, of that he was certain.

The cycloid discs, with a radius of thirty centimetres, bulged in the middle where a digital detonator sensor obtruded. The enigma was, what malevolent genie waited to be unleashed?

The Rani's reply compounded the mystery. 'Let's say they'll change the Doctor's lifestyle.'

'How? Will he suffer?'

A slow smile lit the Rani's classical features. 'Well, I promise you he'll never be the same again . . .'

The joke was too ambiguous for either of her listeners fully to appreciate.

'Excellent. But why not kill two birds with one stone?'

The Doctor's forehead wrinkled; who else was on the Master's hit list?

The Rani did not catch on either. 'Who's the other candidate?' Carrying a number of discs, she was about to exit.

'George Stephenson.'

'How will that threaten the Doctor?'

His explanation was lost as the door whirred shut on them.

How indeed?

Vacating the corridor, the Doctor hurried to the scanner screen control intending to capture the departure of the Time Lords on vision.

The unit refused to function.

'Programmed to respond to her thumbprint,' the

Doctor chuntered.

He wondered whether to chance following after them. But since he was unsure of where the Rani's TARDIS had landed, he could have been exposed the moment the door opened. Opting for safety, he decided to stay put until his adversaries had got well clear.

Meanwhile, idleness was not a characteristic that afflicted him. On the contrary. He delved into his waistcoat for a screwdriver.

' "Gather ye rosebuds while ye may. . ." ' he quoted, although flower-picking was not on the agenda as he knelt under the control console.

14

The Bait

'That Doctor chappie. Strange sort. He was onto something. Try finding him.'

This had been Lord Ravensworth's instruction to the guard. For all his bluster, he was compassionately worried about the condition of Ward and Dobbs. Tying them up was an expedient, not a solution.

Unfortunately, the guard's return brought little relief. 'No sign of Doctor, m'lord, but met his bonny lass.' He ushered Peri into the office.

Clutching at straws, she had come to the mine. If her maverick Don Quixote had any choice, he would certainly show up here, where his own TARDIS was.

Ravensworth was less than polite. 'Devil take you, man! It's the Doctor I wanted to see!'

'That makes two of us!' Peri, too, was in no mood to stand on ceremony.

'You must have some idea of his whereabouts.'

'Must I? He could be anywhere in the Universe!'

'Make sense, girl. Calm down and think. He can't just have disappeared!'

'Oh, can't he!' That was exactly what had happened. One second he was there and the next – whoosh! He'd gone! But how did she explain this to the noble lord? She wouldn't have credited it herself before becoming the Doctor's travelling companion. She smoothed the multicoloured coat draped over the desk, and inadvertently incensed Ward. His struggles and ranting increased.

'The man has to be found.' Anger was tinged with

sorrow. 'We need his help.'

Peri agreed; but, to be honest, she was primarily concerned with her own plight. 'I've more reason to find him than you have! Otherwise I'll have to spend the rest of my days mincing about in these ridiculous skirts!' Collecting the multicoloured coat, she pranced out.

The apparent non-sequitur confounded Ravensworth. 'Do you know what she's getting at?' he demanded.

'Nay, m'lord.' The guard wisely altered the subject. 'Don't seem right seeing Jack Ward like this, do it?'

The recalcitrant aggressor, although almost spent, continued to strain at his bonds.

'No . . . See if you can find young Luke. Tell him we've got his father in my office.'

Someone else intended to enlist Luke's services.

'You're sure you can get George Stephenson here?' Emerging with the Master from the gloom of the old mine, the Rani blinked in the autumnal sunlight.

'Positive. I govern the mind of his apprentice. Lure Stephenson here and the Doctor will come galloping to his rescue!'

The rationale appealed to the pragmatist in the Rani. 'Then give me those. You're wasting time.'

Glad to be relieved of the discs, the Master set off for Killingworth.

On this occasion, the Rani was content to accept his assurances. She recalled that the Master had fed Luke one of her impregnated maggots. Her practical instincts quashed resentment. If their scheme succeeded, she would have to organise mass production of the parasites. Tens, even hundreds of thousands. The magnitude of the operation would necessitate a transfer to where there was an ample supply of the human primates. London? New York?

Laden with the discs that were to launch this grisly

enterprise, she made for a spinny of trees known as Redfern Dell.

'The coast must be clear by now,' the Doctor muttered. Pocketing the screwdriver, he extricated himself from beneath the Rani's console and activated the circuit operating the door.

Outside, darkness greeted him. Nevertheless, he impetuously blundered on – and promptly collided with a loosened pit prop. Dislodged gravel trickled onto his shoulders.

The incident sobered him. An entombing rockfall would not be just a personal tragedy, but a disaster for George Stephenson; more than that, for the whole of humanity. This was not vanity. Only a fellow Time Lord could hope to combat the two pitiless renegades from Gallifrey.

He was jolted from these reflections by a further shower of dust, ominously accompanied by a rumbling groan from the roof . . .

What the heck would she do if the Doctor never returned? Peri sat disconsolately beside the pit shaft nursing the multicoloured coat. She couldn't believe that would happen and yet here she was, shipwrecked. Or should that be spacewrecked?

Sooty eight year old urchins, scavenging for coal, tottered past with heavy baskets. Why weren't they at school, she wondered, then remembered George Stephenson saying he was working down the mine at the age of nine. How romantic the prospect of this visit had been only a short while ago! Now she thought of the mean streets, cramped dwellings and the lack of hygiene. Hygiene? What if she were ill? Medical science didn't exist. Depression making her morbid, she gazed at her leg. Suppose she had an accident and it had to be amputated? Anaesthetics hadn't even been dreamt of!

She'd just have to – what was the phrase? – bite on the bullet –

'Ah, so there you are, Peri.' The Doctor, beaming cheerfully, hailed her.

Relief ignited anger. Peri flung the coat at him. 'Did you come back for that, or me!'

'Both.'

Sulkily, she refused to be humoured. He decided against telling her how near he had been to calamity. Thankfully the invaluable tuition of the Shikari hunters had again come to his aid. Even the barren rubble strewn floor of the old mine bore traces of the Rani's and the Master's spoor, and he had been tutored to detect it. Keen eyes and absolute concentration had got him through the maze of unstable tunnels into the sunlight without further mishap.

'Peri, did you really believe I'd abandon you?'

'So – what happened?'

'Later. Where's Stephenson?'

'I haven't a clue. But Lord Ravensworth wants you in his office. Ask him!'

That seemed a sensible suggestion.

It wasn't. But the Doctor could not know this.

A rasp slipped, grazing Stephenson's knuckle.

'Tha' startled me, Luke! Don't thee know better than to creep up on folk?' He had failed to hear Luke's silent approach as he fashioned a bracket for the Blucher.

Luke's expression did not change. Nor did he respond to the reproval. He had just come from the perimeter fence where he had received the Master's latest directive.

'It's Mr Faraday. There's been another attack!'

Stephenson was sucking the knuckle. 'Faraday? Here in't pit?' How could he be? The meeting had been cancelled. 'Tha's made mistake, lad.'

'Nay, not in't pit.' More pressure was needed. 'He were on't way. Coach were overturned in't woods –'

'Overturned! Is he hurt?'

'Scared, more like. Hiding out, he is.'

Michael Faraday's profound discoveries on electro-magnetism were destined to bring light to the world; provided, that is, destiny remained as written.

'Reckon tha' should go to him, sir.'

'Hiding out, tha' said?'

'In Redfern Dell.'

'Fetch gun for me, Luke.'

Complying – the Master had said nothing about guns – Luke got the blunderbuss from its rack.

'Get thee to th'office.' Stephenson took the weapon. 'Tell his lordship I want all the men he can spare.'

Luke was temporarily disorientated. This instruction did conflict with his mission. But Stephenson, without realising it, resolved the quandary.

'Make haste. 'Tis urgent. I must be off to Redfern Dell.'

Placated, Luke departed.

Methodically, using lead slugs and gunpowder, Stephenson began to prime the blunderbuss. It was a derisory defence for what lay in wait.

Redfern Dell was verdant with wild berries, ferns and grasses. An inviting, peaceful spot.

So it would have been but for the Rani's sinister presence. After setting a dial, she placed a disc on the ground and covered it with leaves.

She moved a pace to the right, then 'planted' the next.

And the next.

Until the halcyon dell was a minefield of the deadly camouflaged discs . . .

15

Metamorphosis

'There's nothing I can do. The men need rest.' The Doctor's dismissal was impatient. Certainly Ward and Dobbs, exhausted to the point of collapse, were pitiable, but he wanted to get to George Stephenson.

'Rest?' Ravensworth did not understand.

'They've been robbed of the power of sleep.'

'Robbed of –? Confound it, man! I don't know what you mean.'

Ravensworth had Peri's sympathy. Decoding the Doctor when he was in this mood would have defeated even an expert cryptologist!

'I haven't time to explain. Peri, see what you can do.'

Turning to leave, he collided with Luke in the office doorway. 'Ah, Luke, is Stephenson in his workshop?'

Luke answered without hesitation. 'Nay, sir.'

'I must find him. Is he at the forge?'

'Nay, sir.'

Luke's laconic manner disturbed the Doctor. 'Did he give you any idea where he'd be?'

'Nay.'

Ravensworth, too, considered this unusual. 'Not at all?'

'Never said nowt, m'lord.'

The Doctor, who had been studying Luke intently, exited abruptly.

A bewildered Ravensworth glanced at Peri.

'Don't bother to ask,' she said, resignedly. 'I haven't a clue what he's up to.'

The Doctor's destination was the workshop. The taciturn replies had convinced him Luke was lying.

'Primed and loaded.' He referred to the blunderbuss tucked under Stephenson's arm. 'You're expecting trouble?'

'Likely as not. I've had message from Faraday. He's taken shelter in Redfern Dell.'

'Message?'

'Aye, he's been attacked. Now out of road, Doct–'

'Luke. He brought you the message.' A statement not a question.

'How did thee know that?' Stephenson found this new acquaintance more and more unpredictable.

The Doctor, typically, ignored the query.

'Stephenson, it's too risky for you out there. Let me go.'

'But Faraday –?'

'If Faraday is there, I'll bring him to you.'

Stephenson's resolve wavered.

'I promise.' The *coup de grâce*. 'You could finish assembling your modified steam bypass.'

'Well – then tha' best take gun.'

'Thank you, no.' However, he did have a parting request. 'Stephenson – I can't explain. But this *is* important.'

'What is't, Doctor?'

'Don't trust Luke . . .'

Luke was indeed a changed youth. Jack Ward, aching from tiredness and unable to sleep, was writhing in the chair, yet his son regarded him almost dispassionately.

'P'raps sleeping draught's t'answer.'

'At least it would sedate them.'

Ravensworth agreed with Peri, but had no means of getting a medicament, short of sending to the town for an apothecary.

'If I had the proper herbs I could make a sedative,'

Peri offered. 'Trouble is, I know nothing about the vegetation in this area.'

'I may be of use there. Somewhat of an amateur botanist myself.' Ravensworth selected a thick volume from his bookcase.

Accepting it, Peri consulted the index then flipped through the pages to the appropriate illustration.

'That's what I need. Valerian. Know it?'

'*Valeriana officinalis*. Matter of fact, I do. It's an indigenous plant. Grows wild hereabouts.'

''Appen I can assist, my lord,' Luke intervened. 'Take Miss Peri to collect herbs.'

'Excellent idea. Just be careful where you go.'

Too true, Peri thought. She didn't want to bump into any of the aggressors who were roaming the country-side.

Lord Ravensworth had no qualms. 'Not to worry, young lady. You'll be in safe hands with Luke.'

'I were thinking of Redfern Dell, m'lord.'

'Couldn't have suggested a better place myself.'

The reptilian embryo's membrane-covered eyes stared fixedly from a jar.

'You saw the apprentice?' the Rani asked the Master, who had come post haste from briefing Luke.

'Yes.'

'He'll get Stephenson to Redfern Dell?'

'Not just Stephenson.' He shuddered with disgust as she topped up the embryo jars with a green, slimy glutinous liquid.

'Don't be enigmatic. It's out of character.'

'I've made doubly sure. He's been instructed to get the girl there too.'

The additional mucus caused the baby dinosaur's pink underbelly to float uppermost.

'Is it entirely imperative for you to do that now?' grumbled the Master.

'Be patient. Stay calm.'

'I've waited too long for this moment to be calm. If you knew how often the Doctor's gone out of his way to sabotage my plans!'

'Only on this occasion he didn't go out of his way, did he? You contrived to get him here.' She put the mucus bottle in a cabinet. 'Force the TARDIS off course, did you? Override the guidance system?'

'Can we forgo the nostalgia, and concentrate on the present!'

'With pleasure.' She activated the external door mechanism. On tenterhooks, the Master barged out of the control room first.

The season of mists and mellow fruitfulness had spread its rich mantle over the woods of Redfern Vale. Squirrels were harvesting hazel nuts and acorns. Ruby-skinned apples and russet pears weighed down the boughs in the lush valley. But it could have been a desolate crater on the moon for all the Rani and the Master saw as they quit the old mine and headed for the Dell.

'Are you sure this plan will work?' he queried.

'I don't make mistakes.'

'If that were true you'd still be on Gallifrey.'

'Experiments are always subject to the unexpected. They can be capricious.'

'Capricious!' he said incredulously. 'Turning mice into monsters!'

'A marginal error. Quickly corrected.'

'The Time Lords didn't think so.'

'Petty spite on the part of the Lord President. Just because they ate his cat.'

'Took a chunk out of him too, I remember! Pity it wasn't the Doctor!'

'That will soon be remedied . . .' The Rani began the steep climb to the ridge above Redfern Dell.

The glory that burnished the landscape was not wasted on the Doctor. Whatever Earth's imperfections – and there were many – he knew of no comparable planet; the inspiration of poets, composers and artists. How could anyone want to desecrate it? He lengthened his stride but kept to the byways. A clash with roving aggressors would put everything into the melting pot.

A vague, almost indiscernible presentiment gnawed at him.

' "Will you walk into my parlour? said the spider to the fly",' he misquoted. 'No, I think not . . .' The Doctor abandoned the path and made a rougher trek through the bracken.

Like a couple of vultures, the Rani and the Master lurked beneath a spreading oak.

'I'd be happier if I could see them.' The Master was chafing at the bit. The vantage point the Rani had chosen limited their view of the clearing below.

'A sentiment they'd reciprocate. We stay here. Out of sight!'

And out of sight they were. Peri, concentrating on looking for the valerian plants, nevertheless gazed up at the great oak cresting the ridge. It was a prime specimen. The botanist's routine desire to classify made her speculate on how old it was.

'Best keep moving, Miss.' Luke was subject to no such diversions.

'Okay, okay. I'm coming.' What was bugging him? She'd conducted many similar expeditions and wasn't about to be hustled by a rookie! She handed him a sample leaf. 'Here. You can't go wrong if you match this.'

'I'm sure I've seen likeness further in't Dell. This way, Miss.'

Vaguely perplexed, she lingered on the outskirts as Luke resolutely led on.

A glimpsed movement at the edge of the Dell alerted the Master. In anticipation, he eased forward.

Delight changed to fury. It was Luke.

He must get rid of the oaf before the fool spoilt everything! Impulsively, he drew the TCE – a hand chopped it from his grasp!

Before the Master could collect his wits, the Doctor had recovered the pernicious weapon.

Thorny brambles had snagged the Doctor's trousers and shredded his sneakers, but the onerous detour had permitted him to circle the ridge, coming up to the rear of the great oak.

In his frustration, the Master berated the Rani. 'So much for your arrogant superiority!'

'A trait you both share.' The Doctor addressed the Rani. 'I got the message. I'm here. Now what obnoxious fate have you conceived?'

'Why me?' she asked.

'He blames you for the failure.'

Her silence mocked him.

'Not this –' The Doctor flourished the TCE. 'That's too simple. You'll have brewed something more malignant.'

But what? Their attitude bothered him as he watched them for any tell-tale signs.

If his attention had not been so fixed, he might have seen Luke sauntering into peril. Instead, the Doctor mentally analysed the facts. He started with the black, frisbee-like objects. What had she said about them? They'd change his lifestyle? Then there was the message that had brought him.

'Is it down there? In the Dell? Where I was supposed to go?'

He glanced down . . . and saw Luke.

But his cry of warning was still-born.

Reaching for a clump of valerian, Luke trod on a disc. Instantly, a fountain of bark-like flakes gushed into the air enshrouding him. Mushrooming upwards, they blocked out the sky, cavorting and dancing on the breeze before beginning to settle.

When they did, two arms were raised in supplication and a brown, corrugated torso was surmounted by swirls and knots that faintly resembled Luke's face.

Where the handsome, golden-haired apprentice had stood, there now stood a tree; a tall, lithe sapling, not adorned with autumn leaves but with the burgeoning buds of Spring. Time was out of joint . . .

16

Life In The Balance

Rage burned in the Doctor's hearts. He levelled the TCE at the Master and the Rani.

'No! No! An accident!' The Master, above all, could recognise murderous intent. 'It wasn't meant for him!'

'And you're so warped, so callous, you think that justifies what you have done!' Never in all their confrontations had the Doctor experienced such an irresistible surge of hatred. 'First you turn an innocent young man into your acolyte, betraying his friends! Then you defile him with this monstrous act!'

'Stop being sentimental.' The Rani felt no remorse. 'What's happened? Animal life has been metamorphosed into vegetable matter. So what?'

'You'll be telling me next he's better off!'

'In essence, he is. A tree has four times the life expectancy of a human being.'

Her Philistine rationalisation appalled the Doctor. He had always harboured a sneaking admiration for the Rani. No more! 'They should never have exiled you! They should have locked you up in a padded cell! Move! Before I forget my abhorrence of violence and eliminate the pair of you!'

A scream.

'Peri!'

Innocent of what had overtaken Luke, Peri had strolled into the Dell. With a 'fool's luck', treading carefully in her unsuitable red shoes, she had managed to avoid the outer booby traps.

Her collection of herbs was sparse until she spied the

generous clump beneath the tall sapling. Red heel poised above a disc, she began to stoop to gather the valerian – a branch of the sapling suddenly swooped, entangling her head and shoulders, forcing her, struggling, back from the disc.

That was when she screamed.

'Stay still, Peri! Stay still!'

Assailed by a tree then, from nowhere, the Doctor's voice, Peri wondered if she was hallucinating.

'The tree won't hurt you!'

She must be hallucinating!

Again the reassurance rang out: 'The tree won't hurt you if you stay still!'

She gave up the fight.

Amazingly, the branch gently swayed aside, releasing her. Despite the personal nightmare the catalyst had plunged him into, the metamorphosed Luke still retained a vestige of his innate decency.

'Perhaps now you'll accept "there are more things in heaven and earth" than your barren philosophy allows!' challenged the Doctor.

The Rani shrugged. 'And perhaps you'll accept you face a dilemma.'

The Master also detected an advantage. 'More of an impasse.' He felt confident again; the moment of danger when the Doctor might have used the TCE had passed.

'Wrong on both counts. There is no impasse. And the dilemma, Rani, will be resolved by you.'

'Get to the point.'

'You put those evil contraptions in the Dell. So, you can lead Peri out!' The Rani shot him a glance of defiance. 'Refuse, and I shan't hesitate to use this!'

The look she gave the Doctor was venomous. But the logic of his ultimatum was irrefutable. Grudgingly, she descended from the ridge, then paused, deep in thought.

'She can't remember!' The Master's evaluation was pessimistic. 'She probably set them at random!'

'I doubt if the Rani's ever done anything at random.' He called to Peri. 'Be patient.'

'But if she has? What then?'

'You're nominated as understudy. I should think you'd turn into a laburnum tree.'

'A laburnum? Why?'

'The pods are poisonous.'

Compartmentalising her emotions, keeping them from impairing her decision making, was a discipline sacrosanct to the Rani. The great leveller, fear, shattered that credo. In choreographed terror, she embarked on a complicated pattern of moves.

Peri's disorientation grew as she recognised the woman in chic leather gear coming towards her. What was the Rani doing here?

Nearing the sapling, another problem loomed for the Rani. There was only a light breeze, yet its leaves were furiously quivering and rustling. What had the Doctor said? 'There were "more things in heaven and earth" . . .' She was going no closer!

'Come to me,' she ordered Peri. 'Keep an absolutely straight line.'

'Tread exactly where she does!' The Doctor meant to sound encouraging, but Peri was confused.

'I don't understand.'

'Stop bleating and do it!' said the Rani. She began to retrace her route, but went too fast, causing Peri to overbalance. She clutched the Rani for support, almost pulling them onto a disc.

The Rani's composure snapped. 'Incompetent dolt! You're worthless!'

'Not to me she isn't! You'd do well to remember that!' The harshness of the Doctor's tone had the desired effect.

With absolute concentration, the Rani continued

weaving a tortuous route among the discs, always making sure Peri was in attendance.

Exploiting the Doctor's absorption in his companion's fate, the Master began surreptitiously to sidle away.

'The next step could be the last . . .' The Doctor's voice was barely audible; his gaze remained steadfastly on the dell. But the Master, who had not heard of peripheral vision, stopped. He did not doubt the threat.

The Rani, also, had halted. 'Can you jump without falling on you face?' she asked Peri.

'Sure.'

'Copy me and you're out of danger.' She leapt, and so did Peri.

'What was that all about?' she yelled as she scrambled up the slope.

'You wandered into a minefield of the Rani's making,' explained the Doctor.

She looked back at the peaceful dell. 'A minefield? In there?' A sudden, chilling thought. 'Luke! What about Luke? Where is he?'

'He just saved your life.'

'You mean Luke . . .? The tree . . .?' The questions were rhetorical as the horror of comprehension benumbed her.

Brusquely, the Doctor waved the TCE. 'Get going. I want you two off this planet before you commit any more atrocities!'

Crocodile-fashion, the four began to file from the ridge.

Strident, ill-tempered laughter emanated from below. A mob of aggressors, some brandishing knives, were trampling through the woods. A dead sheep's carcase was slung from a pole wedged on their shoulders. Obviously it was destined to be skinned and roasted.

'Hurry! Behind here!' The Doctor indicated a laurel

bush.

The Rani had a simpler solution. 'They're easily disposed of.' She extracted the mini-computer from her pouch.

'Give me that!' The Doctor wrested the mini-computer from her.

'If they see you, they'll have no mercy!' The Rani's comment was justified. The aggressors would certainly slaughter the Doctor given the opportunity.

'Maybe not.' He threw the mini-computer to the ground and stamped on it.

'Doctor, they're heading for the Dell!'

Peri's consternation was not echoed by the Master. 'Redfern Dell's about to become populated with new trees . . .'

'Another dilemma, one of morality,' scoffed the Rani.

'And we all know the Doctor's dedication to morality.' The Master could see the pendulum was swinging in their favour.

Untypically, the Doctor prevaricated; risk six lives, or risk genocide? An eternal problem and split seconds to resolve it.

'You have to stop them!' Peri took the TCE. 'Don't worry, I won't have any qualms about using this!' No idle boast. In the past she had demonstrated that she was an expert marksman. 'Get going, Doctor!'

'All right. Take these two to the old mine working. Along this path. Wait for me there.'

'You've got it. Now hurry!'

Pausing only to whisper something to Peri then, seemingly in his haste, colliding with the Master, the Doctor raced off.

'Okay,' ordered Peri. 'You heard him. March!'

With surly reluctance, the Rani led the way. Bringing up the rear, Peri's arm was completely steady. 'And don't try anything! Either of you!'

Peri, to use her colloquialism, was in the driving seat.

The same, however, could not be said of the Doctor.

As he sped down from the ridge, he saw that the leading aggressor, Tim Bass, was about to barge into the clearing.

'*Stop!*' The Doctor's bellow arrested them.

Bass spun about. So did the rest of the gang.

At the sight of the detested inventor, they gave chase. Blundering through ferns, crunching on the thick carpet of fallen leaves, the Doctor decoyed them, helter-skelter, away from the Dell.

At least, that was the intention.

The mob split; a pincer movement that outflanked him. He floundered every which way. Jeering, they made sport of him. All of them had had experience as beaters; putting up pheasant for the gentry. Now they had themselves a sitting duck!

In desperation, the Doctor appealed to reason. Explained how he had rescued them.

They didn't contradict him. They didn't listen.

Relentlessly, the burly, hyped-up hunters closed in . . .

17

More Macabre Memorials

The trio reached the old mine working without mishap, but the uninviting darkness deterred Peri.

'That's far enough!' They halted. 'Now don't move! Either of you!'

Peri's caution was not unwarranted: deviousness was the Master's forté. 'I believe an apology is in order, Miss Peri,' he said. 'I meant you no harm. My quarrel's with the Doctor, not you.'

Peri wasn't having that. 'What about Luke?'

'Luke?'

'Did you mean him no harm!'

'That was *her* idea. Not mine.' Loyalty, for the Master, was a trivial concept.

'Stop grovelling! No-one's going to believe you've got a conscience,' commented the Rani.

'You can hear what she's like.' In apparent agitation, the Master fidgeted with his collar. 'It was her doing, Miss Peri. I didn't even know what she'd planned.' His gloved fingers sought the ribbon around his neck, from which a medallion was suspended.

Suspended by his tethered hands and feet, the Doctor had replaced the sheep's carcase on the pole!

His mission was a failure in every respect. To the accompaniment of victorious acclamations, his bearers were swaggering, once more, for the Dell.

'You must listen! Please! You're making a terrible mistake! I'm not your enemy!'

'Hear that, lads? Mister inventor says us're making

mistake!' That was Tim Bass's reaction from the rear of the column.

Snorts of laughter greeted the remark. The shoulders of the two men hefting the pole rose and sank as they guffawed, making the Doctor's sagging frame swing even more painfully.

The medallion, too, was swinging.

'Put that away!' Peri jabbed the TCE menacingly. 'If you value your miserable life you'll do as I say!'

Crestfallen, the Master complied.

'The Doctor said you'd try to hypnotise me.'

An apoplexy of laughter convulsed the Rani. 'So that's what he whispered before he left!' The laughter changed to coughing. She tried to speak, but the spasm was unremitting. Blindly she fumbled for her pouch.

'Keep your hands where I can see them!' Peri wasn't standing any nonsense. She'd heard about the Master's powers, but the Rani's bag of tricks was unknown territory.

'Only – getting – a – tablet.' Wheezes interrupted her explanation. 'A – nervous – affliction. Won't – stop – without – a – tablet.'

'She'll have a seizure.' The Master feigned concern. 'I've seen it happen before.' His solicitude appeared genuine. Another hacking paroxysm.

'Oh, for pity's sake get the tablet. But carefully. No tricks!'

About to select a capsule, the Rani spluttered again, upsetting the pill box.

Bending as if to collect them, she used the distraction to break a capsule – which she flicked into Peri's face!

Sparkling, iridescent particles were ejected, lacquering her skin so she glowed like a pagan effigy.

Nauseated, swooning, Peri crumpled . . .

'I beg you! Don't go any further!'

Impervious to the Doctor's pleas, the column of bellicose aggressors stormed on.

'Turn back! You're walking into a trap!'

In a thunderous applause of wings, a flock of startled crows flapped skywards as the pole carriers invaded Redfern Dell.

'Stop! Listen to me!'

The leading carrier stomped, confidently, onto a disc!

An explosion of bark-like flakes engulfed the bulky miner in a brown blizzard.

The impact was so abrupt, it jerked the second carrier onto an adjacent disc. A similar fountain of brown flakes mushroomed.

Stunned, the surviving aggressors stared in disbelief at the double transmutation. Where their friends had been there stood two sturdy trees.

Aghast, in disarray, they fled, leaving the Doctor.

But leaving him where?

Still hanging like a sheep's carcase. Only now he was suspended between the two 'trees'.

He took stock of the situation. The pole seemed none too secure. Gently, he twisted to look below. Luck was not with him. Underneath, exposed by the upheaval, was a disc. Any miscalculation and the Doctor's own wooden memorial would be added to the Dell's macabre collection.

He tried freeing his ankles – one end of the pole became dislodged. 'Aaaaaah!'

It fetched up on a protruding branch.

His ill luck had not changed . . . the sloping pole had positioned him directly above the disc. What's more, he was now at an inclining angle, his head lower than his feet!

'Stay calm. Stay calm. It's only a matter of balance.'

Slowly he began sliding his bound ankles towards his bound wrists. Physical dexterity was not his greatest attribute in this present regeneration.

A creak from the near end of the pole. He gulped.

Another slip. His coat tails swept the grass.

Tensing his stomach muscles, he tackled the knot. The fumbling made the pole slip again, bringing his head to within a couple of centimetres of the waiting disc.

Fear speckled his brow with perspiration as he managed to loosen the knot. Gingerly, his soles touched the ground. Keeping close to the 'tree' and away from the disc, he eased his wrists over the end of the pole and untied them.

But his ordeal was not finished. Still marooned, he had to find safe passage through the Rani's minefield.

Unlike Peri earlier, he had no guide. Another lecture to himself. 'There's got to be an answer. Positive thinking's what's needed. Regard it as a sort of board game.' Unfortunately, the penalty for making the wrong move would be grimly final!

Absently, he delved into his cornucopian pockets, and came up empty. Bleakly he contemplated the clearing. Peri would not be able to hold the fort indefinitely. For all her courage – and she was a remarkably brave young woman – she would not be able to cope with the evil pair much longer. 'And then . . . and then . . .' The gruesome prospect acted as a spur. 'What I need is a magic wand.' Wand? His infinite talent for improvisation came to the rescue. Grasping the pole, he extended it in front of him.

Whacking and scouring the terrain ahead, he advanced across the Dell . . .

18

Cave-In

The Rani and the Master were also advancing . . . along the murky tunnels of the old mine towards her TARDIS.

'Wait!' The Master rejected defeat. 'I refuse to run away and let that crack-brained freak win again!'

'Then stay. But without me!'

This did not suit him either. 'Have you no pride?'

'Pride? I'm a scientist. I've calculated the odds, and they, not idiotic pride, dictate my actions.'

'You intellectual microbe! Slave to a computer!' Hardly the dialogue for mutual co-operation! 'He'll be back! He won't desert the girl!'

The Rani was unyielding. 'You'll never learn! Give me my phial.'

'When I'm ready. Not before!' Confidently, he patted his breast pocket.

But for the gloom, the Rani might have registered his fleeting expression of perplexity.

'Peri?' The call curtailed the argument. The Master's assessment had been justified.

Having negotiated the discs, the Doctor's speed would not have disgraced an Olympic champion. His unguarded call, which had been heard by the Master and the Rani, was prompted by Peri's inert, apparently lifeless form.

'Peri!'

She stirred and focused, with relief, on the Doctor's kindly face. 'The Rani . . . tablets . . . my fault . . .'

'Never mind that now. Are you all right?'

'Yes. Yes. I'm fine –'

'Sssh. Hear that?' The scrunch of shale from deeper in the mine. 'The Master's decided to stand and fight! Why couldn't he just have left!'

If this statement was incomprehensible to Peri, the next did little to enlighten her.

'I must get those two into the TARDIS.'

TARDIS? Which TARDIS? Peri, who had been stranded in the bath house when the wardrobe de-materialised, felt her temper rising. Must he always talk in riddles!

'Any chance of an explanation?'

'Later.'

'Later! That's all I ever get! Later!'

The Doctor rattled a pit prop. Firm. He shook another. The same result. The loose prop he had bumped into must be further in . . . where the Master with his TCE lay in ambush.

An all too accurate prediction.

The Master squinted at a bend round which he expected his protagonist to appear. 'Now you see why I didn't kill the girl,' he said to the Rani.

Suddenly, the Doctor flitted across the tunnel, offering himself as a target. The Master fired. Missed. Hit a pit prop – exactly as the Doctor had intended.

The prop glowed red . . . disintegrated.

A slight trickle of dust from the roof . . . A faint rumble . . . Then, eerie silence . . . The Doctor wondered if the stratagem had failed.

An almost imperceptible grinding groan . . . increasing in volume to an ominous rumbling. Grabbing Peri, the Doctor scarpered for the exit.

The Rani and the Master fled further into the mine towards her TARDIS.

Another lull brought the false promise of respite.

126

Convinced the storm would still break, neither of them slowed.

They were not wrong.

A sibilant rustling preceded the onrush of fissures that crazed every surface. The cracks streaked ahead of them in a banshee discord of rupturing stone.

Groping, stung and scratched by slivers of rock, they stumbled blindly on through the mounting cataclysm.

Large chunks of debris pelted them as the roof cleaved apart. Then the inferno took on a new dimension; a torrent of sludge oozed in through the rift, swamping them. Squelching in the rising goo, the quaking Rani thrust the key into the lock of the grey wardrobe.

Indifferent to the Master's plight, she squeezed in the door, not even wanting to offer him the asylum of her TARDIS.

But his instinct for survival was invincible. Before the door could shut, he scraped in.

Refusing to be denied, boulders bombarded the outer shell of the time-machine. Inside, with frenzied discipline, the Rani began the dematerialisation drill at the console.

'Quickly! Quickly! You'll destroy us both!' The Master's accusation enraged her.

'*I* will! You blame *me*?' shrieked the Rani.

Panicking, he leant across the console to operate the controls himself.

Whack!

A mighty wallop sent him reeling!

Winded, he was unable to retaliate as, outside, an ear-splitting tremor released a crushing avalanche. This exterior cauldron of violence was matched by an interior cauldron of seething emotion: acerbic recrimination consumed the dissident pair.

The Rani completed the dematerialisation procedure. All they could do now was be patient.

'You wouldn't be told!' Her shrill voice lacerated him. He alone was the reason they were in this predicament! She would never have delayed for the Doctor's return! She would also have anticipated his cunning and not been suicidally tricked into firing the TCE! When she'd said that the Doctor always outwitted the Master, she was not just goading, she meant it!

A sonic murmur provided respite. The dematerialisation commenced. Above the console panel the silver rings corkscrewed into their intricate intertwining.

Relief brought temporary amnesty.

'Set the co-ordinates for the mine owner's office,' urged the Master.

'Do what?'

'Don't you understand? Run away now and you'll never be free of the Doctor. But feed Lord Ravensworth one of your impregnated maggots, and we'll be able to take over!'

Intuition urged her to reject his advice . . . and yet . . .

'It's the last thing he'll be expecting,' he entreated.

'I'll probably regret this.' She adjusted the space continuum.

'We'll be waiting for the Doctor when he gets there!'

19

Birth Of A Carnivore

'Okay, so what's to stop them materialising somewhere else in Killingworth?'

This was the nub of the issue in Peri's practical mind. She and the Doctor had made their escape. Behind them, huge clouds of dust spumed from the disused mine entrance. Naturally, she rejoiced in their deliverance, but could see no reason for complacency.

She repeated her question.

'What indeed!' The Doctor was twirling a screwdriver nonchalantly. 'While I was in the Rani's TARDIS, I made an adjustment or two.' He chuckled, remembering the occasion. 'To the navigational aid and the velocity regulator.'

Provided it worked, thought Peri. Past experience of the Doctor's so-called modifications kept her in sceptical mood.

The Rani's TARDIS began to vibrate.

'What is it?' asked the Master.

The Rani manipulated the velocity regulator.

'What's wrong?'

'Our speed's increasing,' the Rani replied.

'Then reduce it!' He joined her at the auxiliary power panel.

'You asinine cretin! What do you imagine I'm trying to do!' She elbowed him aside and flicked the velocity regulator again.

No response.

Forsaking that section of the console, she jammed the

navigational aid into an 'off' position. Perhaps that would restrain the unfettered TARDIS.

It didn't.

Instead, in gathering momentum, the room started to rotate . . .

The impact of what was occurring rendered the articulate pair speechless. At this rate of increase, they would cross the frontier into the unknown. No-one had ever travelled at such speeds.

Rotation and acceleration built up to so great a degree that they were being propelled to the walls.

The Rani tried desperately to cling to the console.

It was as if she were submerged in a ferocious whirl-pool, except the suction was reversed. Invisible ten-tacles embraced her. Like unseen leeches, they bled energy from every sinew and muscle, and dragged her outwards. Her clawing fingers lost their purchase. Remorselessly, she was forced away from the console; away from the position where she could influence events. Transfixed against the wall, she, who had re-duced so many to the status of helpless victim, now got a bitter taste of her own medicine.

The vibration had set going a tintinnabulation of tinkling glass as dozens of bottles and tubes jigged and danced.

Glued to the wall, the Master's mesmerized attention was on the Tyrannosaurus Rex embryo jars as they strained their retaining clamps to breaking point . . .

'They're Time Lords, the Rani and the Master.' Peri's prosaic mind worried on. 'They'll repair the TARDIS.'

'Eventually. But not yet. Not before they're beyond the Milky Way!' Exuberance was in every stride the Doctor took as they made their way past the bath house. 'For that matter, beyond most galaxies.' He glanced up at the sky. 'I've heard conditions are rather primitive in the outer reaches of the Universe!'

Glancing skywards too, Peri could not appreciate, as the Doctor could, the real extent of the Rani's and the Master's plight.

'Hardly the setting for an harmonious relationship,' mused the Doctor.

Quite true.

But even he could not foresee how dreadful his enemies' situation would become.

By now the awesome centrifugal force had them plastered against the wall. The resulting 'G' factor was reflected in their agonised rictal grimaces.

Also reflected was terror.

One of the jars had crashed to the floor, ejecting an embryo.

The impact acted as a post-natal slap. The embryo began to squirm . . . it was alive . . .!

Worse . . . it seemed to be developing in size . . .

'It's growing!' The Master's horror was tinged with disbelief. How could the obscenity grow that rapidly? It was an embryo, months away from being fully developed. And yet the limbs and torso were lengthening.

'Acceleration! Time spillage!' The Rani's vocal cords were hoarse with despair. She had seen the Tyrannosaurus Rex in action when she had raided the Cretaceous Age to purloin the embryos. She knew this monster would need to mature very little before it could scrunch them savagely between bone-crushing jaws.

The Master seemed spellbound by the beast as the powerful, arched hind-quarters began to bulge and swell. Its scaly legs grew visibly longer, its talons sharper and stronger. Time spillage was causing the dinosaur to achieve a year's growth in minutes.

Pinned to the wall, even the Rani, with all her brilliance, could think of no counter-measure. They were irretrievably trapped with a creature that would devour them without mercy.

Almost as though it could read their thoughts, the Tyrannosaurus Rex widened its cavernous jaws in a salivating, toothy grin . . .

20

The Final Question

'Where are you going?'

Crossing the pit yard with the Doctor, Peri had diverted towards the office.

'The sleeping draught, remember?' She waggled a bunch of valerian; at least she hadn't forgotten the unfortunate miners.

'Taken care of.' With a smug grin the Doctor produced the phial of brain fluid. 'I managed to –'

'– pick the Master's pocket when you bumped into him!' finished Peri. The Doctor was insufferable.

'Exactly.' He beamed and gave her the phial.

'Well, let me deflate that swollen ego and remind you of something we haven't got – the TARDIS!'

'What the blazes do you think that is?'

'Why not ask t'Doctor?'

Ravensworth raised his eyebrows at Stephenson's reply. 'Have you ever tried asking the Doctor a question?'

Stephenson's smile proved that he had.

As if on cue, the Doctor entered the workshop. He patted the subject of their conversation affectionately.

'Battered but not bowed! Thank you, Stephenson.'

'Had to haul it out manually. T'were no easy task. Took forty men.'

'I'm extremely grateful.'

Arriving, Peri sighed with relief when she saw the TARDIS. Giving Lord Ravensworth the phial of brain fluid, she explained that if he administered it to Jack

Ward and the surviving aggressors, they would recover from their condition.

His lordship accepted the phial without comment.

'No questions?' the Doctor teased.

'My dear man, would there be any point?'

Honours even!

His invention always to the forefront, Stephenson indicated a valve clamped to a vice. 'Tha's a student of science, Doctor.' About to unlock the TARDIS, the Doctor hesitated. 'This valve be t'problem. 'Appen tha' could help?'

The Doctor badly wanted to. Perhaps just a hint? No. Not allowed. Strictly forbidden.

'You'll solve it, my friend.'

'Hope you're right.'

The Time Lord knew he was. History proved it. 'And when you do, your invention will take off like a rocket, Stephenson!'

'Your puns get worse!' groaned Peri.

'Really, Peri? I thought they were improving.' He opened the TARDIS door.

'Er – I will venture one question.' Ravensworth's curiosity had got the better of him. 'What precisely do you do in that box?'

'Argue mainly. Goodbye.' The Doctor ushered Peri smartly inside.

'And don't bother to ask me where I'd like to visit this time!' scolded Peri.

The door slammed shut behind them.

Then, to the amazement of the two men, the light above the police box lit up. Odd sounds throbbed. One . . . two . . . three . . . and the TARDIS de-materialised . . .

Ravensworth was the first to speak. 'I always said he was a strange fellow.'

A nod from Stephenson. 'Aye, where dost reckon he's gone now . . .?'

Epilogue

The bower of mauve and white blossom wafted its scent over the royal party progressing to the greenhouses. Daffodils waved their trumpets, tulips stood stiffly to attention. Spring, in all its glory, was paying a floral tribute.

' "Come down to Kew in lilac time",' recited the Doctor. He had brought them to the magnificent gardens on a sunny April day.

Yet Peri was not overjoyed. She was subdued as she gazed pensively at a purple-bearded iris. The goatee beard and jowl-like petals reminded her of a mournful Cavalier. That was the trouble. Every flower seemed to have a face.

A human face.

But they couldn't have . . .

Could they?

DOCTOR WHO

0426114558	TERRANCE DICKS **Doctor Who and The** **Abominable Snowmen**	**£1.35**
0426200373	**Doctor Who and The** **Android Invasion**	**£1.25**
0426201086	**Doctor Who and The** **Androids of Tara**	**£1.35**
0426116313	IAN MARTER **Doctor Who and The** **Ark in Space**	**£1.35**
0426201043	TERRANCE DICKS **Doctor Who and The** **Armageddon Factor**	**£1.50**
0426112954	**Doctor Who and The** **Auton Invasion**	**£1.50**
0426116747	**Doctor Who and The** **Brain of Morbius**	**£1.35**
0426110250	**Doctor Who and The** **Carnival of Monsters**	**£1.35**
042611471X	MALCOLM HULKE **Doctor Who and** **The Cave Monsters**	**£1.50**
0426117034	TERRANCE DICKS **Doctor Who and The** **Claws of Axos**	**£1.35**
042620123X	DAVID FISHER **Doctor Who and The** **Creature from the Pit**	**£1.35**
0426113160	DAVID WHITAKER **Doctor Who and The Crusaders**	**£1.50**
0426200616	BRIAN HAYLES **Doctor Who and The Curse** **of Peladon**	**£1.50**
0426114639	GERRY DAVIS **Doctor Who and The Cybermen**	**£1.50**
0426113322	BARRY LETTS **Doctor Who and The Daemons**	**£1.50**

Prices are subject to alteration

DOCTOR WHO

0426101103	DAVID WHITAKER **Doctor Who and The Daleks**	£1.50
042611244X	TERRANCE DICKS **Doctor Who and The Dalek Invasion of Earth**	£1.50
0426103807	**Doctor Who and The Day of the Daleks**	£1.35
042620042X	**Doctor Who – Death to the Daleks**	£1.35
0426119657	**Doctor Who and The Deadly Assassin**	£1.50
0426200969	**Doctor Who and The Destiny of the Daleks**	£1.35
0426108744	MALCOLM HULKE **Doctor Who and The Dinosaur Invasion**	£1.35
0426103726	**Doctor Who and The Doomsday Weapon**	£1.50
0426201464	IAN MARTER **Doctor Who and The Enemy of the World**	£1.50
0426200063	TERRANCE DICKS **Doctor Who and The Face of Evil**	£1.50
C426201507	ANDREW SMITH **Doctor Who – Full Circle**	£1.50
0426112601	TERRANCE DICKS **Doctor Who and The Genesis of the Daleks**	£1.35
0426112792	**Doctor Who and The Giant Robot**	£1.35
0426115430	MALCOLM HULKE **Doctor Who and The Green Death**	£1.35

Prices are subject to alteration

DOCTOR WHO

0426200330	TERRANCE DICKS **Doctor Who and The** **Hand of Fear**	£1.35
0426201310	**Doctor Who and The** **Horns of Nimon**	£1.35
0426200098	**Doctor Who and The** **Horror of Fang Rock**	£1.35
0426108663	BRIAN HAYLES **Doctor Who and The** **Ice Warriors**	£1.35
0426200772	**Doctor Who and The** **Image of the Fendahl**	£1.35
0426200934	TERRANCE DICKS **Doctor Who and The** **Invasion of Time**	£1.35
0426200543	**Doctor Who and The** **Invisible Enemy**	£1.35
0426201485	**Doctor Who and The** **Keeper of Traken**	£1.35
0426201256	PHILIP HINCHCLIFFE **Doctor Who and The** **Keys of Marinus**	£1.35
0426201477	DAVID FISHER **Doctor Who and The** **Leisure Hive**	£1.35
0426110412	TERRANCE DICKS **Doctor Who and The** **Loch Ness Monster**	£1.25
0426201493	CHRISTOPHER H BIDMEAD **Doctor Who – Logopolis**	£1.35
0426118936	PHILIP HINCHCLIFFE **Doctor Who and The** **Masque of Mandragora**	£1.25
0426201329	TERRANCE DICKS **Doctor Who and The** **Monster of Peladon**	£1.35

Prices are subject to alteration

DOCTOR WHO

0426116909	Doctor Who and The Mutants	£1.35
0426201302	Doctor Who and The Nightmare of Eden	£1.35
0426112520	Doctor Who and The Planet of the Daleks	£1.35
0426116828	Doctor Who and The Planet of Evil	£1.35
0426106555	Doctor Who and The Planet of the Spiders	£1.35
0426201019	Doctor Who and The Power of Kroll	£1.50
0426116666	Doctor Who and The Pyramids of Mars	£1.35
042610997X	Doctor Who and The Revenge of the Cybermen	£1.35
0426200926	IAN MARTER Doctor Who and The Ribos Operation	£1.50
0426200616	TERRANCE DICKS Doctor Who and The Robots of Death	£1.35
042611308X	MALCOLM HULKE Doctor Who and The Sea Devils	£1.35
0426116586	PHILIP HINCHCLIFFE Doctor Who and The Seeds of Doom	£1.35
0426200497	IAN MARTER Doctor Who and The Sontaran Experiment	£1.35
0426110331	MALCOLM HULKE Doctor Who and The Space War	£1.35
0426201337	TERRANCE DICKS Doctor Who and The State of Decay	£1.35

Prices are subject to alteration

DOCTOR WHO

	0426200993	**Doctor Who and The Stones of Blood**	**£1.35**
	0426200594	**Doctor Who and The Sunmakers**	**£1.50**
☐	0426119738	**Doctor Who and The Talons of Weng Chiang**	**£1.35**
	0426110684	GERRY DAVIS **Doctor Who and The Tenth Planet**	**£1.35**
	0426115007	TERRANCE DICKS **Doctor Who and The Terror of the Autons**	**£1.35**
	0426115783	**Doctor Who – The Three Doctors**	**£1.50**
	0426200233	**Doctor Who and The Time Warriors**	**£1.50**
	0426110765	GERRY DAVIS **Doctor Who and The Tomb of the Cybermen**	**£1.35**
	0426200683	TERRANCE DICKS **Doctor Who and The Underworld**	**£1.35**
	0426201442	**Doctor Who and An Unearthly Child**	**£1.35**
	0426201353	ERIC SAWARD **Doctor Who and The Visitation**	**£1.35**
	0426200829	MALCOLM HULKE **Doctor Who and The War Games**	**£1.50**
	0426201469	JOHN LYDECKER **Doctor Who and Warriors' Gate**	**£1.35**
	0426110846	TERRANCE DICKS **Doctor Who and The Web of Fear**	**£1.35**
	0426113241	BILL STRUTTON **Doctor Who and The Zarbi**	**£1.50**

Prices are subject to alteration

DOCTOR WHO

0426192974	PETER GRIMWADE **Doctor Who – Time-Flight**	£1.50
0426201361	TERRANCE DICKS **Doctor Who – Meglos**	£1.35
0426193261	CHRISTOPHER H. BIDMEAD **Doctor Who – Castrovalva**	£1.50
0426193342	TERRANCE DICKS **Doctor Who – Four to Doomsday**	£1.35
0426193776	IAN MARTER **Doctor Who – Earthshock**	£1.35
0426193857	JOHN LYDECKER **Doctor Who – Terminus**	£1.50
0426193423	TERRANCE DICKS **Doctor Who – Arc of Infinity**	£1.35
0426195108	**Doctor Who – The Five Doctors**	£1.50
0426193938	PETER GRIMWADE **Doctor Who – Mawdryn Undead**	£1.35
0426194578	TERRANCE DICKS **Doctor Who – Snakedance**	£1.35
0426195299	**Doctor Who – Kinda**	£1.35
042619537X	BARBARA CLEGG **Doctor Who – Enlightenment**	£1.50
0426195531	IAN MARTER **Doctor Who – The Dominators**	£1.50
0426195612	TERRANCE DICKS **Doctor Who – Warriors of the Deep**	£1.50
0426195884	JOHN LUCAROTTI **Doctor Who – The Aztecs**	£1.50
0426196171	TERRANCE DICKS **Doctor Who – Inferno**	£1.50
0426196767	GERRY DAVIS **Doctor Who – The Highlanders**	£1.50
0426197801	CHRISTOPHER H. BIDMEAD **Doctor Who – Frontios**	£1.50

Prices are subject to alteration

THIS OFFER EXCLUSIVE TO

READERS

Pin up magnificent full colour posters of DOCTOR WHO

Just send £2.50 for the first poster and £1.25 for each additional poster

TO: **PUBLICITY DEPARTMENT ***
   W. H. ALLEN & CO PLC
   44 HILL STREET
   LONDON W1X 8LB

Cheques, Postal Orders made payable to WH Allen PLC

POSTER 1 ☐   POSTER 2 ☐   POSTER 3 ☐
POSTER 4 ☐   POSTER 5 ☐

Please allow 28 DAYS for delivery.

I enclose £ _____

CHEQUE NO. _____

ACCESS, VISA CARD NO. _____

Name _____

Address _____

_____

*For Australia, New Zealand, USA and Canada apply to distributors
listed on back cover for details and local price list